THE FIRST PEOPLE

THE FIRST PEOPLE

BRAD SHPRINTZ

Bradley Shprintz

Contents

All my dedications are to the readers of my books. There is no purpose without your involvement. I truly mean, from all my heart, that I appreciate your support and hope you enjoy this book.

PART 1

THE DRAGONFLY DILEMMA

Chapter 1

DRAGONFLY

Sam Smith was not elected by the people, yet he had higher security access than the President. He was not known to the public or most people for that matter, the exceptions being only the highest in commands. Having incredible power and still being anonymous is the mark of a wise man. Whether Republicans or Democrats, his title always remained the same, advisor to the President.

He was definitely connected to the well-established military contractors, yet so many more than that. He had information on everyone from sources everywhere. That being part of his power, if there was information you did not want to be exposed, he probably has it.

His career started as military intelligence then the CIA to NSA, and finally, the man between the black projects and the United States Government.

Each President was informed that Sam would be running all the dark projects. Between all the information he had plus resources of the United States Government he was a very powerful man.

People like politicians come and go. Sam Smith always remained in power. It was said you would not see his hand, but you will feel it. Most could not tell you what he looked like or sounded. That was part of his power over people. Like the boogeyman unseen until it is too late.

To the few that dealt with him, he was short with words and always business. That is why the poor soul, now who had to give him the bad news of what just occurred, was worried about being the messenger.

The work they do is never published. For if the public knew about their work, which was combining multiple animal genetic materials together while also creating a new unique genetic code with all the combined traits of each animal mixed, that would surely create a huge outcry from all directions.

Their work was always done in secret, providing the ability to use fewer safety protocols with speed of completion always being important. There were accidents along the process, but in science, that element is always there.

Occasionally an accident brings incredible results that, because of the situation, cannot be replicated. The net result is a truly unique being.

Dragonfly was that incredible accident.

The building was plain, having one story with a flat roof and brick skin. Windowless with a very small parking lot. Most would pass it by without a second look or thought.

Unlike its one floor on the surface, it descended having six basement floors. Each floor had higher security procedures and, what few personnel was there, less access to them.

Once entering the building, the first aspect that seemed odd was the short hallway to another set of doors that were much more reinforced than the doors on the street. The main purpose of this floor was just to process the small number of personnel that entered and left the building.

Dean was in charge of security at the building, working there for over a decade. When working that long in a facility with such high security, he was always a bit paranoid while keeping his thoughts to himself.

His inner thoughts abhorred the place and his job. He was really a prison warden with very few prisoners, and because Dean was human, at some point started to feel sorry for whatever crimes they had committed. In this case, the crime was being created.

They only had one prisoner on the sixth floor. Between her beauty and brains plus special abilities and disposition, she had to be contained, but still, at some level, Dean had pity for her. The life she was born to and now lives were sad.

Dean's inner thoughts were she should have never been able to be created, never been able to grow and survive. Yet through luck and maybe her own will, she was perfect except for her hatred for humans. Not just a hatred but having extreme homicidal tendencies when around any human. That was Dragonfly.

Nina Woodhall had risen above her classmates and then went to the Pentagon. From there, she met Sam and became Executive Director of Operations to the advisor of the President. Being smart and motivated to achieve greatness, she learned a lot from her boss. Unfortunately, these types of calls were part of her job.

Sam Smith answered his phone as he always did with, "Yes." The agent on the other end identified herself, even though Nina knew Sam knew who it was, and proceeded with the following.

"Dragonfly has broken containment. She left a two-word message. It's a name, Brand Wright."

Sam now asked one question with one word.

"Connection?"

"He was the agent that put her into containment the last time she was active. We believe she will locate and finalize him. What would you like done, sir?"

Sam's reply even surprised Nina waiting to follow his orders, "Closely monitor Mr. Wright. When Dragonfly makes contact, proceed with extreme prejudice, regardless of any collateral damage."

There was a brief hesitation as if Nina wasn't completely comprehending what was just spoken, then she answered with, "Yes, sir."

There were very few things that scared Sam Smith. When you have unlimited resources, mistakes, and bad judgments only matter so much. Whether fighting another country or company, there is only so much damage they can do. But Dragonfly was different. She had the one thing that truly scared Sam, incredible intelligence. With that, she could bring down companies or countries. She could change the world as we know it into something totally new.

Sam liked to play chess, and as any chess player will tell you, when you meet someone vastly more skilled in the game, they will destroy you regardless of any advantage given. They can make you feel like every move you make is right until you're checkmated. Intelligence is the most dangerous weapon and the highest regarded commodity. Some would say the only prize worth having, especially when that intelligence is head over heels above the smartest people.

Imagine if Nikola Tesla was allowed to give the world free unlimited energy driving all our technologies wirelessly. Having such advanced intelligence can change the world, countries and companies with no one being able to stop it. That is why it must always be controlled or nipped in the bud before control is lost.

As his thoughts were justifying his actions, another issue crossed his mind. Brand Wright's file was displayed on his computer screen. As he continued to review the file his thoughts followed. This man was a very useful agent. More than half his missions he was unaware of because his mind was wiped of those events. But even so, Sam was impressed with the number of missions, and successes Brand had. Just in the last year, he combated a demon, killed a vampire, survived aliens, and met with a jinn. That is when he saw the connection to Mr. X. If he proceeded with his last order, the balance would be changed. Then again, Brand Wright, aka Mr. X, is old and will die at some point soon.

Sam did not like wasting words or assets and definitely did not like disrupting the established order of things. Even when you have more assets than needed, he was troubled knowing that to effectively destroy Dragonfly, an explosion would be needed or at least most effective. And using Brand Wright as bait was the most efficient way to get her, with the probability of his survival being extremely low.

In the end, after two times being in a maximum-security containment unit and escaping, the threat of what Dragonfly could possibly do was worth the price of Brand Wright and whoever else would be in the way.

Chapter 2

IT BEGINS

Hector was born to be a realtor, at least, that is what it seemed. Since getting his license, he and his wife sold more homes in one month than seasoned professionals do in a year. Being he spoke English and Spanish fluently, and his mind was sharp regarding numbers, that with his positive personality, he quickly became a superstar within the ranks of that profession.

But extreme success comes with a price, even if your bank accounts are overflowing with money. Having a complete dedication to sales, regardless of whatever it takes to make that happen. Usually, that would mean breaking the rules or guidelines that others would not do. In this case, he received the phone call right before he was going to head home. The night's sky had that Florida twilight, which contains gorgeous colors consisting of purples, lavenders, pinks and reds.

"Hello, sir. Yes, this is Hector. How can I help you?" The man on the other end was polite. Human nature seems to feel that if someone is polite, they must be a good person. Of course, this is not the case, and maybe it only applies to certain people's human nature. After, arrangements were made to show the home, which the polite man almost demanded be done as soon as possible. Tonight, if not right now!

Hector was tired and definitely did not need the sale, but his motto was, being willing to do what others would not do. So even though he was tired, the thrill of the next sale was like an enticing aphrodisiac.

Hector was armed, and though he was on the smaller size, he had heart, a lot of it. So there was no fear as he drove in the darkness with only the full moon to shine light. The main roads of Florida are somewhat well lit, but the crossroads, which can extend for miles, have only the light you bring plus what the sky is willing to provide.

No one knows what his thoughts were, if on the pending sale or of future pleasure elsewhere to be had. Maybe thoughts of the past, which by the passing of time, make them all the sweeter. Once arriving at his destination, his future client was nowhere to be seen.

The development of homes was on the high end. Seemingly in the middle of nowhere, but that is how new areas are developed. First, you start with the rich, that are happy to see no poor homes near their community. Slowly the wheels of progress plus human needs surround and make their way into whatever wanted paradise had started.

The home he was showing was located at the edge of the new development. The homes were spread apart from each other with more than enough room to never know your neighbors. As Hector was waiting by the front door, checking his watch and thinking about leaving after 10 minutes, all of a sudden, the atmosphere changed.

It was now pitch dark with only the full moon plus the stars shining. They seemed to Hector to be brighter than he ever remembered. Then in an instant, the fear started. An unreasonable fright that something awful was about to happen. He felt his gun which was now fully out and in his hand. Yet the fear became worse. For a moment, he laughed at himself and was just about to walk back to his car, to write this possible sale off, leaving it for another to complete.

The attack started with some bushes moving unnaturally against the wind. Then the entire form rose up to be fully seen. Hector was looking at something from mythology. Knowing it should not exist and also knowing that he would die that night, he spoke these words in Spanish. Actually, speaking is the wrong terminology; they were yelled at his opponent, filled with an anger knowing his death was imminent.

He was able to shoot two rounds before the creature ripped half his throat away. Unfortunately, the first blow did not instantly kill Hector. He did not live much longer than that, yet however long was too long. The creature just kept ripping Hector apart with a hatred for its victim that was demonic.

When the police arrived, his phone, wallet, and keys were all found. His car was still sitting where he parked it. Robbery was ruled out quickly, but with the severity of the injuries, even just being a murder was questioned. Why would someone go to the extent of ripping a person apart just to kill them? The case was well documented by the police, being so unusual. Hector had made a lot of friends; even some officers at the scene knew him. Everyone involved wanted answers and, of course, no more murders.

What will never be known to the investigators were Hector's last words, "¡Brand te matará!".

Chapter 3

SAD NEWS

Bubba was a big southern businessman. He was very shrewd when it came to generating wealth. He had started small, but with great investments plus diversification and then time, his monetary worth was quite high. The reality was that he never let it get to his head. He was able to gain a nice fortune while still staying himself. That is not easy to do.

Once someone gains power, money or fame it can be hard to ever stay who you really are. Some regain themselves, but it may take decades or extreme sorrow. Others die or never get back to the better person they were.

Bubba had just heard the sad news and thought of his good friend, Brand Wright. People rub off on one another, and as Brand had said, there are some things that just need to be said face to face. So, without calling first, for he knew Brand would be able to know something was wrong from his voice tones. He would just show up and give his old friend the tragic news in person.

Sad drives like lonely walks remind us how fleeting things are. Bubba recalled how just a year ago, Hector, Brand, and himself were the three musketeers. Now that seemed so long ago.

There is always a moral injustice when people younger than you die. Hector was the youngest in the group of friends. Then again, there is the thought that whether you're 4 or 94, it was your time. Either way, it was a hard drive for Bubba.

The thing is, everyone takes the news of someone close who dies differently. And when it came to Brand, he was always hard to predict. Whatever Bubba was thinking, he did not expect what was coming.

Brand Wright stood 5 feet 10 inches, with an olive complexion. His 64 years belied the public, being that he still had hair and it was of a dark brown color with very little grey near the ears. Being of average build, it was his eyes that truly fooled people. They were a cool blueish grey fire that brightly focused on whatever subject they were observing, making them hard to look away or tell lies to. Brand's eyes gave him strength, a power others did not have.

He had worked as a spy with the military, moving around the world. Being trained to infiltrate, he quickly felt comfortable in other countries and people he worked with. He had many life-or-death situations, some having someone else die instead of himself. After a time, it changes a person, to only wanting peace.

Now he was retired and appreciating the simple joys of life, which are given freely for those who have the senses to perceive them. He was outside with Sweetbull, his best friend. They ate, played and slept together. The love between them was strong, for they only had each other, and deep down, they both knew it. Sweetbull, being a blue nose pit bull, her only fault was having too much love for people.

They were fighting over a tired six-foot braided rope, which was stiff at one point in its life. Now it was super flexible with Sweetbull and Brand having a tug of war over who would get the prize.

Bubba's unplanned arrival brought joy to his old friend. Of course, Sweetbull was aware first and started the run to greet her friend, with Brand following her trail. Brand's mood of late and especially that day was the simple joy of not being in too much pain. Able to enjoy things like eating, walking, and peaceful contemplation. To most, that would seem like basic things not to be cherished. Being old it's different. Being able to enjoy simple things is not that simple.

In reality, the more Brand was removed from people, the happier he became. Of course, his small group of close friends were an exception to the rule. Bubba and Hector had made it to that group, and Brand was better for it.

Brand greeted his friend with, "Hello Mr. Bubba, you hungry? I haven't eaten anything?"

Bubba responded, "Yes, sounds good. I have some bad," and then modified it with, "Sad news."

Now Bubba had Brand's full attention. Brand's eyes locked onto Bubba's eyes, observing every feature on his face, listening like each word was life and death. This only made it harder for Bubba to get the story out. He dropped his head slightly, lowering his voice almost to a whisper. It seemed like his large frame had shrunk as he told the tale.

He began with, "Hector died last night while showing a home. His funeral service is on Friday, and I was thinking we would go together. I will pick you up, say two."

Brand seemed frozen for a second like his mind was evaluating each word that had been spoken. To Bubba, Brand's whole body seemed to change. Maybe he was standing a bit taller, he had lost 10 pounds since the last time the men met, but Brand seemed to look bigger proportionately than just a few seconds ago.

Brand's response was cold and commanding, "How did Hector die? Please provide all the details you know, regardless of how inconsequential they may seem."

Bubba continued, "I was contacted by my friend who's a cop. He stated that there was an unusual murder at the new development called Sweet Dreams. He knew Hector and knew we were friends, so he gave me the heads up."

Again, Brand's attention was fully on Bubba. He responded, "Unusual murder? Did he provide details?"

Before Bubba could answer, Brand's next statement was more like a demand, "Contact your friend and have him provide everything he knows, preferably in writing," and then, as an afterthought, "As soon as he can!" Now again his attention was on listening to all the current details Bubba knew.

Once Bubba told all he knew, he tried again to pacify his old friend.

"Brand, we all miss Hector. I know you're upset. Let's eat. Lunch is on me," he said with a big smile.

Brand, who now had no interest in eating, answered with, "Thanks Bubba, but I am not hungry. Actually, I have some things that must be done right now. Thanks for stopping over."

Now Bubba started to feel hurt but continued, "Well, what about the funeral? Should I pick you up?"

Brand replied, "Actually, I have a meeting with a man named Big Bill. I will attend the funeral first and then find out what this fella wants."

Bubba looking at Brand, kind of in shock, said, "You don't know who he is. One of the meanest killers out there, the gangs- heck, even the police don't mess with him. He kills people for the mob and runs a protection business. Someone you definitely don't want to mess with!"

"Thank you, my friend, but right now, I am someone you don't want to mess with."

Bubba now started to get angry, "We are all mad about poor Hector but going gangster isn't helping."

Brand now looked long and hard at Bubba, like he was evaluating each word in his head for accuracy. "I dedicate my life to finding whomever or whatever killed Hector, and I will destroy them."

Bubba had seen many facets of his friend's personality. He now realized he never saw Brand mad. It was like a cold breeze on a cold day. He seemed to have more energy, to be bigger but at the same time more inside himself regarding expressions and words spoken.

It was like all the time before, Brand had been the immovable object, and now he was the unstoppable force. Bubba had seen things happen around Brand that, if retold, most would think him crazy.

Bubba closed in, saying, "I will contract my friend and get all the information I can in writing and report back to you ASAP."

Brand shook his head ever so slightly up and down and marched into his trailer.

Chapter 4

CHAMELEON

Hector was a good man and a close friend. When they met, he was doing odd jobs and just working the street. But after he met his wife, his whole life changed. Now he was a very successful businessman that supposedly was in the wrong place at the wrong time.

Brand was not buying it. His gut feeling was telling him that what was known and what was told were two different stories. This killing had not truly reveal its nature. Whatever killed Hector, whatever that may be, was his last and only mission in life, to remove this vile evil from the planet completely.

As Brand's thoughts roared on about Hector, he also realized that subconsciously old people don't want to make new friends because they are already carrying so many gone souls. There is a chance, even with younger people, that if befriended, they too may soon have to be carried with all the others.

Brand was a retired spy, but right now, he felt like he did in the old days, across enemy lines. The power and the fear all blended into a drug that could not be bought or gotten. It tunes up your senses, so sounds and sights all have meanings.

Roy and his family owned the land that Brand's 5th wheel resided on. They let him stay there with no land charge. His expenses were electricity and a satellite dish. Roy had always been kind, but last year Brand found out why. Right now, getting Hector's killer was all that mattered. Hector was a good friend. Roy had ulterior motives, and maybe he was kind, maybe it was just an act. Either way, Roy was working for a man named Bolt who was using or at least monitoring Brand.

Sam Smith usually had numerous issues to deal with. He had grown accustomed to being patient when needed. Nobody enjoys waiting, but there are times when physics or life events make it happen. Stressing over it will not make it any quicker. Most of the time, what he wanted happened faster than for any other person on the planet. But this time was different. Finding a needle in a haystack would be a thousand times easier. The needle doesn't disguise itself and move away from being located when searched.

Sam thought of the great ones in the spy business. Mata Hari was at the top, she was working for multiple countries, and no one knew who she was really working for. Dragonfly's abilities made her look like an amateur. Dragonfly spoke five languages fluently, but maybe more, could change her looks like a person changing their clothes. Above all that, her intelligence was off the charts.

Sam's last report on her current location went as follows. Nina Woodhall, who Sam was mentoring, communicated she could be in Asia or Europe, possibly in the USA or Mexico, but we feel strongly that she is not in Australia or Russia, but that is not a certainty. With her abilities to speak the language fluently wherever she was, combined with her great disguising techniques, she never stands out. The reality is she could be working at the Pentagon and we still don't know. We have been monitoring Brand Wright but have not had any sightings of the two together.

In Sam's mind, if she is taking time it means she is setting something up. Or maybe creating something. Bottom line is the longer this takes the worse things might get. Being very powerful but still in control of yourself with that power, Sam thanked Nina and told her to double her efforts in completing the objective.

Then he contacted Lieutenant Colonel Bolt, who was in charge of the RB program. Brand Wright was known as Subject 9 in that program. Sam smiled to himself on how so many things go full circle. It was just last year Bolt had contacted him about a zombie issue, which was easily resolved. Now he was contacting Bolt to inform him of the current problem with Dragonfly and how it may affect his Subject 9. Maybe Bolt had some information not in the system, meaning not on computers, and talking with him might shed additional information.

Sam was like that, being very thorough in approaching highly critical matters. He liked Bolt and his security clearance was close enough to what was needed that it would not be an issue. The real truth was Sam was scared. Deep down, he felt if anything could harm him, it was this. A rogue super-genius that has a deep-rooted hatred of humanity. And the deepest truth was that his name was all over Dragonfly's life, from her creation to both high-security containments. If anyone could find that out, it would be Dragonfly. And if she did, what would she do to him?

Brand Wright sat in his rig, Sweetbull registering the change in her friend. She had tried to comfort him, but she could tell he would have none of it. She watched, ready to help when needed. Brand looked at his right arm from the inside wrist, rising past his inside elbow, then finishing an inch below his shoulder. It looked like a tattoo of a short Roman sword, having a black, highly polished blade that started at the wrist. It changed to the handle once past the inside elbow, having a marble black and white finish. Notwithstanding the image itself, it had a wet 3D look to it. Like something never seen before if you really examined it.

And of course, looks are very deceiving. Its real name will never be known. Brand referred to it as Chameleon.

Its origin happened near the beginning of the Universe. There was an element formed which was extremely rare. This element spent millions of years before it became self-aware. Exactly how many are in the Universe is not known, but there are only a handful. It's ability to manipulate time and itself has limits. Like a battery, after major feats, it needs to recharge. Unlike a battery, it is self-recharging with the passage of time.

In regards to its shape, it's just a form it takes. Like all of us, it is composed of energy plus frequency and vibrations, except it could modify all those properties. Even with all that power, it at times becomes lonely. Hence that's where Brand comes in.

Their union formed in the prior year, as Brand was fighting Gabriel Hand, a two-thousand-year-old vampire. What a man will do in battle reveals a lot about who that man is. It was in that battle that Chameleon chose Brand, for, with Chameleon, it always did the choosing. Regarding the people Chameleon chooses, from their perspective, it must feel very powerful to have that type of power attached to you at all times. The bottom line is that they were two separate beings but traveling as one.

Brand needed information. Now with Darrell gone, who used to provide that type of thing, he was perplexed. Here he was ready for the battle, at least mentally, but where was the enemy? Patience is needed for war, just as it is needed for peace. So, for now, he went over his weapons, making sure he had plenty of rounds. Knives were sharp and the battle armor was in good shape. If only he knew what killed Hector and where it was located.

For already, with what little details he had heard from Bubba, he knew this thing was not human. Maybe it was the demon they fought together last year? Deep down, Brand thought not. That demon enjoyed tormenting its victims. This felt like it was done quickly but with pleasure. The irony was maybe Hector just was in the wrong place at the wrong time.

Chapter 5

THE FUNERAL

The funeral had a huge crowd. That is the way it seemed to go. The older you were, the smaller the group. But if you died young, well, there are so many that want to say goodbye. To Brand, it seemed to reflect life. In youth, there are so many friends and family, but as time marches in its never-ending fashion, so few are left at the end.

There were many groups that appeared to want to go into the funeral parlor, and even though it was their largest, it was inadequate for the task compared to all that came. Friends comprised one large portion, and then there were the realtors. They were another large group. Of course, there was the family and their friends. There were even people like Bubba and Brand. Hard to figure out where they fit in Hector's short life, but they also wanted to pay their respects.

Because of the crowds and the fact that it was so depressing to be inside where the casket was displayed, it was a closed casket. There were, however, many beautiful pictures of Hector in his glory. It really always feels wrong when a young person dies. The injustice can never really be balanced. The best that can be done is if it was a murder, catch and kill the killer. That hardly is justice. The soul lost is a tragedy, period.

At the last funeral Brand attended, he was crying over the loss of his good friend Perry. A tragedy, yes but by disease. Something that cannot be caught and killed. This funeral was different. Brand had a hard look, like someone that has seen death so much it no longer affects him. Inside it was much different. His anger about Hector being killed seemed to inflate him with energy and drive him with one singular goal. Life becomes easier when all one's focus is on one objective.

In Brand's case, it was to find and destroy his friend's killer, nothing more and nothing less. He will not be distracted or discouraged until his mission is complete. Being at the funeral only reinforced that goal.

Bubba and Brand were about ready to leave and head home, for the funeral visit was to pay public respect, there would be no going to the home to mourn. That has always been a private affair for Brand.

As they were shuffling through the outside crowd to get to Bubba's truck, a young lady approached. She introduced herself as Joy, who had come from Puerto Rico to visit Hector. She was young, maybe 25, with long dark hair. Very shapely, her face had a sweetness with a smile that instantly said, "Let's be friends."

Now when it comes to gifts, one must always accept them. Brand had been to many foreign countries, and it is terribly disrespectful to refuse a gift. It says either the gift or the giver is not worthy, which is considered to be a huge insult to the giver.

Brand, to his credit, tried to be respectful, but Joy persisted, and of course, he had to accept all that was given. There was a lot of stuff. Bubba went to her car to help move all of it or, as she put it, "Everything in the back seat and truck, please. Thank you so much, Mr. Bubba." With that sweet smile, that would be hard to resist for anyone.

As Brand and Joy talked alone, this is what was said.

Brand looked deeply into Joy's eyes and asked, but it was more like a statement, "Why are you really here, bringing all this stuff?"

Joy seemed not rattled at all and replied, "Hector sent me a text saying that if anything bad happened to him to see you, Brand Wright." She continued, "He respected you more than you know and told me to bring gifts and to help you. You're going to find his killers, yes?"

Brand had been listening without expression. It seemed like no matter what she said, it would not affect him. Being in that zone where you hear and see but do not feel. It happens when you have one objective.

Now he realized he was supposed to respond and, without moving a muscle, said, "I will destroy whatever killed Hector. I dedicate my life to this one purpose." Now it was Joy's turn to seem frozen, not that his words surprised her but just the power that Brand was now emitting. Joy gave him her number and a little hug, whispering in his ear something in Spanish that he would never know.

Sam Smith was listening to Nina Woodhall, about the news regarding Dragonfly. Usually, he did not interrupt as he had mastered the willpower to listen. In this case, it was obvious Nina had let him down, and the instinct to reprimand was too strong.

Nina was telling him that they may have had a sighting of Dragonfly at a funeral that Brand attended.

"We were not 100% sure, but there was a very high probability. Joy is the cover name she was using, and they were together for a brief moment. It was a very crowded funeral. She did not try to terminate Brand."

Sam could stand it no longer, he knew she was not done, but he had heard enough to lose his temper, which did not happen often.

"How long were they together?" Sam said it sternly, and the silence was awful.

Nina responded while checking her report, "Seven minutes."

Sam answered, "Plenty of time. You have the appropriate teams on ready, triangular approach with hand missiles."

Nina replied, "There would have been high collateral damage. In my assessment, too high." She said that with conviction, but it was the wrong answer.

Now Sam was looking at her like when someone is evaluating you during an interview.

He started, "This is all off the record, agreed?"

Nina responded, "Absolutely."

Sam looked into her eyes, "Do you know the difference between a killer and killer instinct?"

Nina answered with a textbook answer which Sam actually interrupted her.

"No, I don't want the definition. Do you know the difference? I can tell you don't. Let me try a different way. Is killing someone and telling someone to kill someone the same thing?"

Nina now looked conflicted, "Yes, I believe it is."

Sam again shook his head, looking down like he was sad, which he really wasn't.

Sam, now looking Nina in her eyes, stated, "You have never killed anyone with your hands or by pulling the trigger. It is easy to tell. There is no difference between a killer and a killer instinct. But there is a huge difference between killing someone personally and telling someone to do it. I don't know if you're up to what needs to be done, maybe a reassignment or a vacation?"

Now Nina responded cause she could take no more. "The next opportunity I get there will be blood, sir. I will not let you down."

Sam shook his head slightly up and down and said, "I will give you one more opportunity, don't disappoint me."

With that, Nina was dismissed to let Sam enjoy the recent events. Feeling happy with himself that he has provided enough motivation for Nina to get the job done. Though it was bittersweet in that she could have resolved the problem right then and there.

Then he reviewed her report more closely. Nina was top of her class. If she wasn't, she would never have risen so far. He had no doubt there would be blood.

Question, why did Dragonfly not kill Brand at the funeral? The report said to put him off guard, and probably their next meeting, he would meet his death. Sam knew that was wrong. If Dragonfly wanted Brand dead, she could have easily done it at the funeral.

She was showing herself to him. Saying she is right here, in the game. And she figured that we would not kill her there. That is the problem with a super genius. They are always many steps ahead. She now figures that we know and will try to kill her the next time she is spotted. Sam was playing right into her hand. At least, that is how he felt. That is the problem with playing against an opponent in chess who is far superior. You keep thinking you are making the right moves until they beat you.

Sam sat in thought, thinking I am missing something important that is right in front of me. Then it came into his mind like it had been there all along. The report said Hector was torn apart. Brand's profile suggests he would want revenge. I will lead Brand to Hector's murderer, and if Dragonfly really wants to protect him, she will show herself. Even though it sounds crazy, he would not be playing her game.

There are times in chess when you create a distraction that has no purpose but to take the other player off their game.

Sam continued his thoughts. Then if she does show, we can get two birds with one stone.

Chapter 6

THE RB PROGRAM

Colonel Bolt had oversight of the reality bender program, or RB, to most who are in the know. Being recently promoted from Lieutenant Colonel to Colonel had changed his plans on retirement. He was amused at himself on how a title change can make such an impact to his future.

Science is often misunderstood. There is so much known and so much unknown. Even when it is unknown, it still can be manipulated to our needs. Take light, it acts like a particle and also like a wave. The problem is waves have no mass, and particles do. Still not easily explained or fully understood. Yet it can be used in many ways without a true understanding of how it works.

Gravity fits that class, too. Its properties in the subatomic world are nothing like the world built upon it. Of course, these issues and so many more are widely documented but rarely read by the public.

The RB program had that type of conflict. There are individuals who can force the laws of physics to bend to their will. It is different in all subjects that possess it. The effects are usually very minor but still should not happen.

They can be studied, and the effects observed, yet the reasons why some people have that power and others don't are not known.

Brand Wright had that power. It was subtle but definitely there. Colonel Bolt had been observing Subject 9 for a long time. He would never say his name. Bolt believed that even mentioning a subject's name could cause a link between the two. RBs affect not only physics but also the emotions and actions of the people around them.

The call from Sam Smith always has to be answered. And even with his position as Colonel, Sam Smith was the boss. The problem with Dragonfly takes priority and using Subject 9 as the bait makes good sense. But Bolt had grown a friendship, like a guard to a prisoner, with Subject 9. More than that, he had an unreasonable faith that somehow Subject 9 would defeat not only Hector's killer but also Dragonfly. Subject 9 had been able to put her in containment the last time, who knows.

Chapter 7

BIG BILL

Bubba met Brand at his rig and began transferring all the stuff Joy had provided to Brand at the funeral.

Bubba asked, "When you going to meet Big Bill? And don't go to the deck in the back. He runs that restaurant, heard-"

But before Bubba finished, Brand replied, "In an hour, and I am supposed to meet him at the deck in the back," which Brand seemed to grin, like something he was looking forward to.

Bubba resumed saying, "Then I am going with you. They probably won't kill us both if we are together."

Brand responded, "No, Bubba. If this fella is as dangerous as you make him, I will not put you in danger, period."

Now it was Bubba's turn to lay down the law, "Then I will follow you to the restaurant and wait at the front until you return from the deck!" It was said as no discussion would follow or be accepted.

The compromise was accepted by both men. Bubba inquired whether Brand would be carrying a weapon and that they would check him before he entered the back deck. There is a corridor that runs around the side of the restaurant leading to the deck in the back. Usually, there is a guard at the beginning of the corridor from the restaurant and another at the exit of the corridor to the deck.

Brand went over a plan to get by the first guard. When Bubba asked about the second, Brand gave that look. The look said he won't stop me. Brand had gone into a different mindset than his friend had ever seen him in. It was very intense, but even more surprising was its longevity, the total natural nature that Brand displayed it with. It wasn't an act but seemed like his core being. Bubba thought to himself, if this were an act, his friend was the greatest actor he knew.

The restaurant was in a nice part of town and on the higher end regarding the meals and bills. Truth was, Brand had no idea what Big Bill wanted, at one point thinking maybe he wanted Brand to do some type of work for him. But the invitation was demanding and left the taste that it would not be a pleasurable experience in both not showing up or showing up.

Curiosity can be a dangerous thing, Brand wanted to know why he had been requested, and the quickest, easiest way was just to show up and deal with it. That, of course, was before his friend had been killed. Now Big Bill was getting a totally different man. It can only be wondered how differently that meeting would have gone if Hector had never been killed.

The restaurant's front seating area had few customers and Bubba was half correct. There was a man guarding the entrance to the corridor to the back deck. The entrance to the deck off the corridor was empty with no guard. The man guarding the entrance to the corridor was big and looked well seasoned in regard to violence.

Big Bill created his empire with terror and brutality. His reputation for getting the job done, especially in regards to murder for hire, and just his general disposition of being angry and dangerous. He created a protection business for steady income, but it was the extra jobs that were exciting to him. He also liked mentoring young men that were similar to his nature, violent and strong. To help them with their craft, that being to hurt and intimidate their targets. Lastly, to avoid the mistakes he made in his youth.

Tiny was one of those youths. He was huge and strong, but even more importantly, enjoyed the violence he inflicted. Having no hesitation to engage in combat was an important plus when Big Bill evaluated the new crop of wannabes. The ones that had potential were placed in little gangs to gain experience. Once ready, they would be moved to different crime families for a tidy profit.

With Big Bill, it was more than just the money in regards to training young men to be killers. He felt like it was his duty to his profession. When he heard that Tiny was seriously injured by a man who he had no beef with. Not only that, but that man hurt Tiny with a piece of paper. That was just an insult on top of the other facts. It really bothered Big Bill, but he was a business man. At the time, he was busy with real problems that were directly connected to his business. Then he became distracted with other matters but making things right never left his mind.

He wanted to meet Brand to determine if he should seriously injure him or kill him. When not being paid to kill somebody, Big Bill would make his mind up about killing somebody right there on the spot. Might be something the victim said or some factor that would make Big Bill decide.

He had called for the meeting with Brand Wright to determine if death or just an injury was in order. Most of his men were on other business so he just had his personal bodyguard plus his man at the corridor entrance. Even with how he hurt Tiny, Big Bill did not expect much from Brand. By the end of the confrontation, that question of death or injury would become quite clear.

Chapter 8

MEETING BIG BILL

Bubba and Brand entered the restaurant together and then split up until Brand was approaching the corridor to the deck in the back. As Brand was walking straight towards the corridor, making clear eye contact with the guard, Bubba approached quickly from the left. The guard responded to Bubba by moving a half turn his way and taking a step to the left. Bubba always knew how to play his size. Being a large man, it always worked in his favor.

Bubba grabbed the guard's left arm and, with his strength, was able to immobilize it for the few seconds that would be needed. Brand moved at that exact moment Bubba grabbed his left arm and was able to negotiate around the guard and into the corridor.

Brand was now marching toward the entryway into the back deck.

A large table to the left of the corridor's exit on the deck, sat Big Bill.

There was only one other man in the room, who looked like a bodyguard from his size and demeanor. Big Bill was mean and angry, as was his general nature, yet he was not impulsive. He planned his actions with controlled details.

Big Bill spoke loudly and with total authority, "Put both your hands on the top of this table and do not take them off from the table until told to do so."

Brand looked at him with that smile that he had of late. A smile that said trouble is welcome, very welcome, and I will not be deterred. Brand walked to the table with both his hands up, palms facing the men. Brand slowly sat down while placing both palms on the top of the table as instructed.

Big Bill stared at him for quite some time, which only heightened the tension that had started with Brand's entrance.

Finally, Big Bill said, "Explain why you attacked Tiny when you had no business with him?"

Brand looking confused, "Tiny? Can you be more specific? Who's Tiny? When did it occur? What actually happened?"

Now Big Bill looked annoyed, "It happened about a year ago. You hit him in the throat. He found God after your encounter."

Brand, looking like he was bored, responded with, "So what? Let me tell you something." As he said that, he started to rise from the chair he was sitting on. His hands were still planted firmly on the table, but his body was rising and leaning toward Big Bill.

Brand continued, now being less than a foot from Big Bill's face. "I am part of the baddest gang there is, Uncle Sam, US Government. If a flea on my dog dies, if anyone that I care about has an accident, you will only wish for death or jail. My people will destroy your little group of merry men but you-" At this point, Brand now put on a big smile and continued.

"You, they will put into a test tube. Yeah ,they have them that big. I have seen the faces of those locked within those tubes. You don't know what despair looks like. You will wish for death, but they'll keep you alive for a long time. You don't have a chance against me, harm me, and you'll be destroyed."

Now he rose completely up, taking both hands from the table and stating, "This meeting is done." Brand started walking calmly without hesitation to the corridor leading to the front and exit of the restaurant. When he was within five steps of the entrance to the corridor, the command came from the table behind him.

Big Bill roared with anger, "Stop right there!"

Now Brand spun around, taking half the steps back towards the spot he had just left. He was taking large, swagger steps, with the last step looking like he was going to fall on the table in front of the men. Right before that step, Brand had slid his hand between his loose-fitting shirt and pants. Pulling the revolver and cocking it in one motion, it was now pointing at Big Bill's head.

Brand, now visibly upset, said, "You have not been listening. Now, if your friend here breathes hard, I am feeling twitchy. Bill, you'll be the first to know if that happens! You want to end it right now?"

Then for a moment, there was silence as Bill's bodyguard took in what was happening. Brand had a gun less than a foot from his boss's head, and with what was going down, he did not want to make a mistake. Bill's bodyguard had his gun out but was looking at Big Bill for directions.

Brand who at this point was well past the point of no return, again demanded if Big Bill wanted to end it now.

Big Bill finally responded with, "You can go. We will meet again!"

Brand responded, "The next time will be the last time!" With that, he started walking backward toward the corridor with his gun still pointing towards Big Bill.

Just then Brand realized that Bubba was walking toward the guard at the corridor's entrance towards them, his gun aimed at the back of the guard. At the point that Brand and Bubba met eyes, Bubba stopped moving while the guard continued. It felt like an exchanging of prisoners. Once Brand reached Bubba, they started to move out of the corridor and to the restaurant exit. Brand walked backward with his gun facing their enemies while Bubba had his gun on their path to freedom.

As Brand and Bubba made it outside, Bubba was visibly shaken.

"He's gonna kill us!"

Brand was thinking with that smile that said, trouble, I am looking forward to it. But then, looking at his very good friend who had risked his life to save him, now the burden of that deed was haunting him.

"Bubba thank you for all you do! We will be fine, and you're welcome to stay with Sweetbull and me."

Chapter 9

MORE
INFORMATION

Colonel Bolt had received information regarding Hector's killer from Sam Smith's top person, Nina Woodhall. She had detailed information regarding the killer's location, phone number, and other information that the government should not know.

Bolt had to transfer this information to Subject 9, of course, he would never do it in person. Actually, he did not even want to use one of his agents to meet Subject 9. People who have contact with him, either good things seem to happen, or their life starts a downward spiral. He decided to have an agent feed Bubba the information, and Bubba, by his nature, would bring it to Subject 9.

In regards to the extent of information the government has on each person that resides in America is mind-blowing. That, with algorithms from computers, can predict where you will go on a Tuesday, what you will eat and wear, who you will see, what roads you will take, who you will text and call, how many times you will go to certain websites, etc. Big Data is the term used by the people who deal with that type of information. It's the power to predict so many aspects of a person's life. Well, if the general public truly understood, there would be a revolt in data collection.

Bolt had done many things in his career that he either disagreed with or just did not want to do. After decades of giving and following orders, after all the internal arguments are fought, a soldier will just follow orders. No matter what he feels, that is his job.

To lose Subject 9 on a chance that Dragonfly might intercept, he knew it was a long shot. Finding someone who is a professional at not being found, sometimes the easiest and only way is to draw them out. Dragonfly was that important, and he understood that it made sense. Still, he hated doing what he was doing.

After Brand left the restaurant and headed home, trying to think he had handled it well, yet knowing that was false. Still, it was enjoyable. He was on a mission to find Hector's killer and to destroy it when encountered. It was simple, and everything else did not matter. All other distractions needed to be eliminated.

It had been a long time since he had given that type of speech. It always felt good when given and usually had the desired effect. This time it would work against him. In truth, he just did not care. What was bothering him was the lack of anything useful to find the killer.

Bubba had transmitted all the information he could get from the police. There were some interesting facts but nothing to locate where the suspect was. As Brand's mind was focused on facts, connections regarding the different aspects started to develop into a theory. Yes, a crazy theory but something to cover the facts as currently known. Bubba declined Brand's offer to stay at his place. It had been about 2 hours once Brand was home that he received the call from Bubba.

"I have some hot info. It's on paper. Can I stop over?"

Brand thought his prayers have been answered.

"Yes," and then in afterthought, "Thanks."

Bubba arrived shortly after his call. Unlike his last visit to Brand rig, this was all business.

It seemed to Brand that Bubba had now taken on in a form his current persona. Hard and tough with danger just strengthening the bond.

Brand began, "How do you know the source that gave you this information?"

Bubba replied, "Well, I don't know him. He called me, said he had hot info on the Hector killing, and heard from the cops I was interested."

Brand continued, "So how much did he want?"

Bubba now was looking confused, "He didn't want anything?"

Brand seemed upset, "He did not ask for money or anything?"

Bubba shook his head from side to side, saying no without words. Then as if he was thinking about it said, "Now that you say it, it does seem strange that he did not want money. I assumed he was a friend of the cops and was just trying to help, but- "

Brand interrupted him, "It does not matter. Either the info is good, or it's junk. Either way, it needs to be checked out! Just seems very fortunate for me to get- "

Bubba now interrupted, "Us to get that info. Don't even start 'cause I am helping you find and kill Hector's killer. He was my friend too."

So it was settled that they would together sort this out to its final conclusion. But Brand had told Bubba that he would see things Brand would do that would change his opinion of him and some things that he will never be able to forget, bad things. Brand tried to warn his friend that he would show no mercy when the time came.

Big Bill now was on a mission. He had been punk out by Brand, who had gotten the better of him during their first meeting. It had been a long time since Big Bill had a real passion for something. Most things were just a job or having fun at someone else's expense. This was different, it was like he was woken up from watching a movie, and now it was time for him to fix things.

In his mind, this town, heck, the country, is not big enough for them both. There can only be Big Bill or Brand Wright, not both. Before their meeting, it was about whether Brand gets a beating or death. Now, death without question, but it would have to be himself killing Brand.

There was a small voice telling Big Bill to let it go. What if he is right, and you end up in a test tube? But that voice was very small, and his pride and ego could never let this slide. So Big Bill started to plan, for even though he was mean, he was not stupid or impulsive. This killing would need a very good plan because the only thing left in Big Bill's mind was the killing of Brand Wright, and how great it will feel afterward.

Brand was thinking about the statement, two enter and only one is able to leave. It is the ultimate test a person can give themselves. As failure is not an option. When everything is on the line, all your senses are on high alert. There is no future just now. Being so close to death makes life much more real.

Gaylord Fisher was a good man, well, as good as a man can be. All men have secrets, shades of their persona not revealed often to others. Some have secrets that are so bad that, if known, would destroy all they have created. Guarding those secrets becomes imperative.

Gaylord helped the community he lived in and most of the people around him. He was one of the top bankers at a small community bank. Having the ability to approve loans that others would not while still making good financial decisions made Gaylord very liked and wealthy.

His secret was a big awful one, seemingly matching all the good he did by having one thing that was terrible. He was a good man, and to him, it was an affliction, a disease that made him innocent of any damage he inflicted.

Each time he transgressed, he would do some special extra good deed to amend for it. There are some things that cannot be made right. No matter how many good deeds are done, there has to be a reckoning.

Sweetbull was concerned about her friend. Brand's blue nose pit bull had given him space. The change in his attitude made her feel she had done something wrong. Now Brand had to snap back to his other attitude, the one that Sweetbull knew. And for a short time, he went back to the friend she loved. They played and then ate and then played watching YouTube together. Brand knew that when he would awake in the morning, he would be Hector's avenger again.

Brand could hear the phone ringing in his head, which was the sign Chameleon wanted to communicate. He answered it within his mind, and it began.

Chameleon saying, "Time is so different for you compared to me. It is hard for me to understand how you endure it!"

Brand responded, "That shortness is a gift in more ways than seem apparent. It makes everything important! It pushes you exactly because it is short. For that matter, don't you ever just get tired of existence? Don't you at some point want to know what is next, if there is something next?"

Chameleon answered, "Your kind just can't understand how long time is. That is why you don't appreciate how terribly short your existence is. Imagine my world with a bird that picks a pebble and then drops it in a certain spot every 100 years. Pebble by pebble each 100 years until they form the biggest mountain in your world. Then imagine a bird every 100 years taking one pebble from that mountain. When the mountain has disappeared and looks exactly like it did before that process began, that is one second of my life. Compare that to the short time you have. How does it not make you angry?"

Brand did understand his question, for he felt that way about Sweetbull. It hurt him that Sweetbull's life was so short compared to his own. Yet it never bothered Sweetbull because it is all so relative. The injustice of some things was hard to rationalize. With the standard answer being it is what it is.

Then he thought of Hector's short life, heck his life was more than twice Hector's time here on the planet. Hector had more money, friends, possessions, and a loving wife. Yet the one thing that kept it going, time, he was short on. Brand's thoughts went to his own 64 years, twice more than Hector, but how little they really added up to.

Truth is Chameleon and Brand were so different that neither could really understand the other's perspective. Even with that, there was a true friendship that existed. They enjoyed their conversations and appreciated each other. Sweetbull, Chameleon, and Brand did have one aspect in common, they each were alone and only had each other to share that loneliness with.

Brand had to admit that the information Bubba had supplied him was very good. It was too good. It felt more like the professional report he was used to in his field days for the government. Having information that was way to personal that only the most intimate might know. He had a good feeling that this was his man, but maybe man is not the right term.

Given that the event happened on a full moon, the victim was ripped apart for no apparent reason, and there were patterns of similar but not publicized situations. It seemed the only satisfactory conclusion was he was dealing with a werewolf. Even when he rationalized it in his mind, it sounded crazy. Even with all that he had already seen last year, it still sounded crazy. Yet it fit all the facts to a T.

So research had to be done to destroy this thing. Many times he had wished recently for Darrell's help. But Darrell had gotten himself killed over greed last year, and all his research would have to be done on his own.

People were taking their time but plotting how to attain their goals.

Big Bill was mainly thinking about after he killed Brand, he would go underground for quite a while. He had already setup a base in case the police or something would make his days numbered. Now he was making sure he had enough supplies and proper communication channels to run his business but, for all purposes, be invisible.

Deep down he had a bad feeling about killing Brand. That this will be his battle of Waterloo. That he knew this would end badly, so he just needed to disappear for a while. Time has a way of making the past be forgotten as the present is always demanding attention. After Brand was killed and a good amount of time had passed, he would reappear. The killing of Brand would be easy. His thoughts and plans were about after that event.

Brand Wright was planning on interrogating Hector's killer, Gaylord Fisher. He wanted to know every truth that was associated with Hector's death. Once he had retrieved as much information as he could get, then he would kill Gaylord. His thoughts were about how to trap him. Also, he wanted to do this during the next full moon in case he had any doubts. If he did he would wait till then before acting. Having a good plan for a situation that has so many variables is always needed.

Brand's state of mind knew that he would improvise most of the capture, but he would make a good plan to kill the monster. That was the essential part and point of the mission.

Nina Woodhall was planning on not missing the next opportunity to kill Dragonfly. She replayed in her mind Sam Smith's prior instructions. Especially the part, regardless of any collateral damage. The next time she will instruct the teams to double their firepower. Nina was ready to be a killer. In fact, now it was in her blood. She was almost as anxious to get the call as Sam Smith was.

She knew her entire career rested in completing this operation. She had much bigger plans than being one of Sam Smith's top agents. She pictured herself as President, and people like Sam Smith could make that happen. She would not fail when her next opportunity came, she thought to herself with a smile. There will be blood.

Colonel Bolt almost always seemed to be planning something. Currently, he was trying to figure out a way of helping Subject 9 without getting caught. Something he could do to ever so slightly tilt the outcome to a favorable conclusion for Subject 9.

Sam Smith was thinking about how close he was to resolving this abnormality. To him, he was playing a chess game and had the opponent's queen cornered. He was just two moves away from capturing the queen, a metaphor for killing Dragonfly, without losing his queen in the process. Once she was eliminated, he could continue on with his world dominion plans.

And then there was Dragonfly. What was she planning? What was her end game? That no one knew. She was the proverbial wild card, the rogue who could change everyone's plans.

Synchronicity is an odd or amazing thing depending on your perspective, especially when it leads to a singular event.

Big Bill had one of his men plant a tracker on Brand's bike Matilda and had been observing his movements for the last two weeks. He had a plan that involved himself and one of his younger better, looking killers. The actual killing should be simple, and then the real plan goes into effect. He would disappear from the public and electronic tracking devices. Going actually underground to a base he had set up in case of a possible planet extinction event.

Now that two weeks had passed and he had more time to think about it, he was pleased with the decision. He needed a change. Everything he was doing now seemed more like a chore than excitement and fun, which it was in the past.

Going underground was new and had that unknown excitement that truly new experiences bring. Also, he wanted to read more. As time had marched through his life, he had changed.

Many would call it the mellowing out that happens when a person grows old. Now, if you ask that old person, he or she would just tell you they got smarter, and you'll understand when you age. Big Bill, at 67 years old, was getting more religious and wanted time to study without having people around him, period.

So he was ready and excited to kill Brand and get to his new life. The sting of their last meeting was still sore. It will feel so good when he sees the look in Brand's eyes. That look like this is the person who killed me. Big Bill wondered if he would have that surprised or sad look.

Brand Wright had a plan. Back in the day, they would call it a PIP, plan in process. That means there is somewhat of a plan, but there are still many failure points that need to be resolved. The problem of getting Gaylord where he wanted him was actually quite easily solved in his mind.

Spies use influence and threats but rarely brute force in making something happen. Others might try to strong-arm via guns or actual violence to get Gaylord to meet them. Or they may try to ambush or just do a plain frontal assault on their target. Not spies, the way of a spy is to entice your victim by many different means, so they do what you want without any physical force.

Getting Gaylord to Brand seemed easy in his mind. It was the after part that was a work in progress. Before he killed him, he wanted answers, even if he already believed he knew them.

In one week, there would be another full moon, and that is when he would make his move. That way, there could be no mistake when he would see it with his own eyes.

Nina Woodhall was monitoring Brand now with great intensity. She was ready and better understood the risk that Dragonfly presented. She had a General that was at her command to facilitate whatever actions were needed, and they were on high alert for her call.

Sam Smith's talks with her affected her more than was apparent. Nina was mentally ready to actually kill someone. She believed that it showed the top players that you are in the game. Actually, she had contact with many people who personally had killed people while being top people within the government. This would be her step forward to be noticed for her dream of being President Woodhall.

Brand was thinking about what he was going to do when he and Gaylord met. Really about killing people and how it changes you. His thoughts went as follows: The first time you kill someone, it is usually hard, if not physically, then mentally. The second is much easier then the first. And so it goes, given enough time with that much blood on your hands, you know you are going to Hell. The truth is you are going right after the first one.

Chapter 10

GAYLORD FISHER

Gaylord Fisher worked with many developers. In most businesses, finance is king. Without it there is no business, or if there is a business, it will not last long. With it, dreams can turn into reality, and failures can be saved. Like blood is needed for the body, money makes everything happen, at least in the business world.

Today Gaylord was giving his approval for the loan request of a large new community development. That is after he suggested and it was added many improvements. A children's playground, dog park and dog grooming station, and a nature walk path.

Gaylord held the keys to the money, so his suggestions made things happen. He was pleased with himself. Knowing that he made differences for good, especially ones that last a long time. Even though he worked with money, he really enjoyed working with his hands. Building things or planting trees, actions that would last long past his time here on earth. He felt that if everyone here just left the earth a little bit better than when they arrived, after a bit of time, it would be a utopia.

In the very back of his mind, he knew he had one week before his curse would afflict him again. He had tried different approaches to conquering the sickness. That is how he referred to his problem as his sickness. And his victims were referred to as his medicine. So soon, he would need more medicine to survive.

His thoughts never went to the philosophy of whether his life was worth taking another. Or if they did, then obviously, he thought he had more right to live than his victims. His pity only went to his affliction and his conscience to paying its way to freedom.

When he first became affected, he would travel far each month for his medicine. Over time given that feeling of being untouchable plus just laziness had made his medicine pick-ups become relatively close to his home. That along with perfecting his mode of operation, he would lure his victim to a secluded spot where he could release the pressure of needing to kill. Cause that was really what it was. He did not steal from nor did he eat his kill. Once he had performed the act, it was like his body released a chemical that relaxed him and let him have the peace he so desired.

So new plans would have to be made for in seven days, the full moon would appear, so would the affliction and the finding of medicine be needed.

In any operation, there is a level of planning. Starting sometimes with the cover story and working the way back to all the actions needed for success. Many times it is in the little details. The added second and third options at critical stages that are the difference in avoiding failure.

Brand did the planning for the mission taking place in less than a week. Obviously, there were the clothes needed, with everything being in black. That included the face mask and hat, gloves, socks, and shoes. Bubba and Brand would be wearing identical outfits, but those were the easy details.

Of course, they had burner phones, which are mostly un-traceable. A car that was bought a while back and had no history to them. Those are the easy details, the hard ones, if not taken care of, are the ones to get you killed or caught. And then there were the weapons, guns, a lot of guns. With silver bullets made in all the different sizes needed for the guns associated with them.

Brand also brought a chain with two padlocks, the plan being to chain up Gaylord and wait for the full moon. Just before he changes totally, Brand and Bubba would shoot him dead and cut off his head, just for good measure. Then, of course, to escape before anyone becomes aware of what happened. There were many holes with the plan.

Brand tried his best to get Bubba not to go or at least just stay in the car and be the driver. He tried to explain the importance of having a driver who is not involved in the action. Adrenaline can be both a marvelous help and a terrible disaster. Once the deed has been done, it is very hard to act and be normal. Yes, it can be done, especially with practice, but if things go bad, well, adrenaline and driving are not a good mix.

Bubba would have none of it. Brand still planned on trying when they arrived at the home of their target.

The day was rainy, which made Brand think about his Grandmother. It had rained at her funeral, and he remembered hearing someone say that the Angels were crying. That, plus the general gray scenario, gave him a gloomy feeling, none of that mattered.

Bubba was driving, and nothing was said as they drove the fifty miles to the target. Brand had his game face on, but really it was more than that. It was a mindset, nothing would stop him. Death was not feared. If it happened, then that was meant to happen.

There is peace even when tremendous violence is just ahead. A peace of knowing that what you are doing is right. There is no doubt or worry about what will be done. Peace knowing that when it is done, if you survive, you have accomplished what was needed, period.

First, they parked by Gaylord Fisher's bank, just watching the people going in and out. Brand had known many rich people in his life, and for all their wealth, their moral code was non-existent. It is easy to do the right thing when you have the money available to do so. Unfortunately for the people who don't have that luxury, they have to compromise their actions.

There were the rich and poor all meeting together at the shrine of money. And the king of that building was Gaylord Fisher. His power and reach helped most who entered it. There he was loved as a kind gentleman.

The truth was far from that, and everything Brand was watching reassured him the first part of his plan would work. The second batch of information Bubba had received was very detailed, which Brand would be using in two hours.

Next they drove to his home, which was in a gated community. Bubba punched in the code retrieved from the information he gotten from some stranger trying to help. Brand knew it was more than that and most of his plan relied on that information being accurate. The gate opened without incident.

Security is really just a state of mind. Homes have windows, and if you really want an entry that is just like an unlocked door. Even locks can be picked quite easily and really provide no security. Animals are the best first alerts but will never stop someone with guns and bad intentions.

True security is done in layers, with each layer adding to the probability that you will be secure. The more layers, the greater chance of survival. Most homes have four or five layers before vulnerability occurs.

That consists of locked doors, animals, and or alarm systems, with guns and knives as the last resort for the home dwellers. If they are really smart, they will also have a safe room in their home. Each of these systems can be beaten but obviously, the more they have, the safer they will be.

In today's world, people try to eliminate the human element. No one trusts their neighbors. Families don't trust their own members. This is actually a huge mistake. Having a human element within the security framework that you can trust is a huge asset.

Gaylord had an electronic lock and security system, which brought him peace of mind. No dogs, housekeepers, or even a wife or children. He lived alone in a very big home with neighbors quite far from his view. It could not be more perfect for Brand's plans.

It was around 2 o'clock pm when Brand and Bubba arrived in the driveway and started to approach the door to Gaylord's domain. And as if the fates of fortune were on their side, the electronic lock was opened by pressing the right number sequence. Then the alarm system was deactivated again by pressing the correct numbers required. It was all going too easy.

After doing a quick inspection of the home to ensure there was no one else hiding, Brand continued with his agenda.

Next on the plan was the phone call, which if worked, would draw Gaylord right to them. This was the most difficult part besides killing him. If it did not go well, the mission would be defeated.

Brand used his burner phone, which he had loaded all the information he thought would be required. He dialed Gaylord's private number, gotten from Bubba's information. As soon as the phone was answered, Brand began.

"Hello, Mr. Gaylord. I am your friend. Please listen to me carefully. I am sending you three pictures in text messages, look at them and then delete them. Have you received the text messages?"

Gaylord, who was now flustered, replied, "Yes, I have."

Brand continued, "Good, now delete them. I will wait."

Gaylord responded, "They are gone."

"Good, now all I want is some information. I am not a black-mailer, just someone who has an incredible curiosity. But I am not someone to be toyed with! It takes 21 minutes to get from your bank to here. I will give you 25 minutes to be here. If you take 26 minutes, I will be gone plus much more information will be posted on the internet and on TV. All I want is information, and then I will be gone. Do you have any questions?"

Gaylord's voice now was different. It was low, like someone who has been found guilty and now can barely speak. "Where is here?"

Brand knowing he had his target, replied with cockiness, "Well, in your home, of course!" And with that sent a fourth text message of a picture in Gaylord's living room. Brand then added, "I have 2:22, and you have 25 minutes to get here." With that, he terminated the call and prepared to wait for the show to begin. He thought, usually, when things go too right, it is the setup for things to go terribly wrong.

Bubba now was looking a bit pale. Things are very different when you are actually a participant than watching a movie or playing a video game. He was a brave man, but these types of situations are tough, even for veterans who do these things.

Brand was smoking heavily but seemed quite collected. The trick was to always be ahead of your target. At least one step but preferably many more than that. Real control does not involve coercion. It is making the target do as you request because, in their mind, there are no other options available.

Gaylord arrived with three minutes to spare, running to the front door and then walking in slowly. Brand was in the foyer waiting, and Bubba was standing by the door on the left side. After he entered, Brand started to speak.

"Mr. Gaylord, how nice of you to entertain my curiosity. But first, just for my own protection, I ask that you allow me to secure your legs so I will feel more comfortable." With that, he produced the chain link and padlock that was in his bag.

Brand continued, "Mr. Blue with take care of this minor thing, and then we can begin. Once I have all my questions answered, I will let you go, and we will never meet again."

Now Bubba had taken the chain and padlock from Brand and started to approach Gaylord.

There are times when your enemy is in a weak state. There can be a number of reasons, but the effect is always the same. They reside themselves that this present fight is over, but there will be another round. Gaylord was processing everything but did not have a plan to stop it currently. He assumed these men had guns, and even if he killed them now, the information they were holding over him still could be exposed. He would play his weak hand for now, knowing he had a wild card coming.

Bubba attached the chain links around Gaylord's ankles, making it as tight as he could, and then applied the padlock. At this point, Gaylord needed to sit down, so they helped him to the formal living room on the left.

Brand's plan had so far gone perfectly, which can lead to letting your guard down. Now he was at the point, except for killing Gaylord, that he really wanted to be, getting answers.

When interrogating someone, you want to be friendly. If it is done with torture, most of the information obtained is unreliable. Bubba was sitting on a couch, but Brand made him move because his back was to the window. Eventually, every-one settled down in their spot.

Brand began, "How did you acquire your current condition?" Brand was very careful to be friendly and not mention any negative attributes. This technique of interrogation takes time but can be very effective.

Gaylord seemed to feel more relaxed and responded, "I was driving on a rainy night, and my tire had a blowout. As I was fixing the flat, some animal attacked me, and then the animal was attacked by a gang of men." Then adding, "I imagine they were chasing it, and that saved my life, but also changed me. You understand it is not my fault. I am a victim."

Brand had told Bubba not to speak at all while in the presence of Gaylord. So as the exchange continued, Gaylord's eyes were solely on Brand.

Brand acknowledged with a head nod, a sign of approval, and continued with questions. How long has he had the "problem" and all types of questions like that. After what seemed like quite some time, hours really, Brand finally got to the questions he really cared about.

"So why did you pick Hector?"

Gaylord responded that he was just in the wrong place. That got Brand angry, or at least that is the impression he was conveying.

"You're lying, I know you're lying, and we were getting along so well. All I ask is that you tell me the truth so I totally understand what happened."

Gaylord looked confused, so Brand continued, "You called him and lured him to that place. You were going to kill him! Yeah, even with your burner phone, I know it came from you." Now his tone easing again, trying to be a friend.

Brand said, "All I want is the truth, and I will set you free, so I ask again, why did you call Hector? Why him?"

Gaylord now reverted back to being compliant saying, "There was a mansion deal that would never have happened without a balloon mortgage. No one would process it except me. That deal happened because of me, and the buyers could not thank Hector enough for making it happen. I made it happen. At one million two hundred thousand, Hector made a fast 36 thousand and no one thanked me."

Now Brand who did not seemed fazed asked matter of fact, "So you killed him because no one thanked you?"

Gaylord seemed to finally get angry, giving Brand a look like he was an idiot and shouted.

"I was jealous of him! He was the talk of the town. I was jealous and figured I could get rid of him and have my medicine. Are you happy now that you have the truth? He was arrogant and flashy, but the people loved him. I helped them for years, and everyone talked about Hector. I am a good man and do much good for everyone around me!"

Brand seemed happy and said, "You see, I told you the truth would set you free. Doesn't it feel better to let it out? Our work here is done, Mr. Blue. It's time."

Just as Brand was going to his backpack to get his weapon of choice and as Bubba was also now arming himself, four men appeared in the open double doorway to the living room. They were all dressed in the same gear and had a plan.

Time has always been a fascination with Brand. Many times he would look at his watch, focusing on the second hand, and was sure it had stopped. Then after what felt like at least two to three seconds later, it would start and continue as it had never stopped.

Brand always wondered whether he sped up which made the second hand look like it had stopped, or did time just slow down for that moment. Either way, the effects were the same. During that time that the second hand seemed to be stopped, Brand could think many more thoughts than in a typical second. This effect had happened even before he ever met Chameleon.

The four men burst through the open doorway with two men moving to the left and one moving toward the right. The last man held his position within the entry to the living room. Then the man standing in the entry shot what must have been a .45, hitting Bubba in the chest. Knocking him through the wall residing behind him. Bubba was killed so fast that, to Brand, time felt like it had stopped, like in the past when looking at his watch's second hand stopping, he would have an extra two or three seconds to react than the rest in the room.

Now thinking clearly, he aimed his gun at the man in the entry who had just killed Bubba. He shot one round, which hit and removed his jaw from his face. Brand also had a gun with powerful bullets. The man was still alive but now looked like a horror movie character and in a state of shock. There is a panic look that the eyes reveal when they know all hope is lost, Brand was looking into those eyes right now. He went down to his knees, between the blood lose and shock he would be dead soon.

With the last of Brand's extra seconds, he turned his attention to the man closest to him as opposed to the two men across from him. The man was so close that extending his arm and lightly tapping the killer's extended arm was enough when time caught up to them. His shot missed, and then Brand's second shot of the night struck him between the eyes. He was dead before he hit the floor.

It started with an unnatural sound making the remaining men left look towards that direction. Then as if being mesmerized, Brand could not look away or think of anything else but the change. The cracks and pops as bones and skin grew, hair becoming thicker and longer. Yet worse than all else was the transformation of Gaylord's face as it was growing in size, with large teeth and little black dots around a red liquid for eyes. An abomination is just a word until it transforms from a human to a monster. Last was the smell of rotten potatoes, plus a death smell.

Brand was brought back to reality, hearing the two men across from him start shooting the creature. It made a movement that was so fast it looked like it teleported to the men shooting at it. With savage sweeps of its arms, finger nails more than an inch long, ripping the two men apart. They were already beaten, trying to fall to their deaths, yet the creature just kept ripping them with their blood flying about.

Brand started shooting; now he had a gun in each hand and was not aiming, just shooting in the direction in front of him. One of his silver bullets hit the werewolf in the upper thigh. The werewolf let out an animal cry that hurt the ears while scaring the soul, it left the room and crashed through the back door.

Just then, Bubba started to move and made an awful groaning sound. Brand spoke out loud, "Thank God you're alive." He rushed to his friend, who was wearing a bulletproof vest which saved his life.

Bubba was now regaining his senses and feeling the pain more clearly. Brand instantly had a change in plans and now wanted Bubba to leave immediately. He helped him up and was telling him to drive slowly and get to checkpoint A. Then changed transport and dump the clothes and go home.

Bubba was now looking around at the horrific sight. The man without the jaw was close to death now laid out on the floor not moving but still making sounds. Some people take a lot longer to go than others. The other three men were quite dead. Bubba looking at Brand asked, "Dear Jesus did we get him?"

Brand responded, "No, he got away, but I will kill him! You need to go. I have things here I need to do. Drive slowly and follow the plan." Bubba not wanting to leave his friend, only Brand's insistence forced him to go.

Once Bubba was in the car, and the taillights had faded into the dark, all of Brand's power seemed to fade with them. Now he had the opposite of adrenaline, whatever that is called. Blood was everywhere, especially on Brand. There is a lot of blowback when shooting someone not to mention a werewolf ripping two men apart.

Brand had made a promise to himself last year that there would be no more blood on his hands. Now he had just killed two men with his target getting away. This could only be classified as a complete failure. He was mad and disappointed with himself. He was prepared to die but wanted to kill Hector's killer first.

Everything was going so well and according to plan, and his mind was now trying to evaluate where he made his mistakes. There were some positive things. Bubba did not kill anyone and had escaped this problem. Gaylord's confession about killing Hector, so there is no doubt who has to pay for that.

Brand just was not moving. He was sitting in a room consisting of now four dead men and with no energy or motivation to leave. In the back of his mind, with all the gunfire, leaving quickly is vital to his escape, and yet he did not move. As his thoughts went on, he really messed this up. He should have killed Gaylord after he captured him. Once the shootout started and seeing Gaylord's transformation was too much. His mind was saying that he was too old and being so sloppy he deserved whatever was coming for him.

Just then, the noise outside brought the chatter within his head to silence. It was the police, but it seemed like more than that. Even with that, he did not move, just waited for his punishment.

Chapter 11

CLEAN UP

Sunday was the epitome of a great employee. His every breath, action and thought were on his job. His pride and dedication to being an FBI Field Commander showed with his total commitment to that responsibility.

He was alerted that there may be some action at the address of Gaylord Fisher. The exact nature and details of the upcoming event were not known. Being prepared and ready for action Sunday and one agent had been sitting in their vehicle up the street of the address, waiting and watching.

There were many shots fired from multiple guns, and then some minutes later, one very large animal burst through the back door of the home. After some more time, they observed Bubba leaving Brand from the front door of the residence. That is when Sunday drove down to the home and was now parked in the driveway.

He was waiting after hearing the police were coming to intercept them and then secure and investigate the scene.

Sunday had an average build, but his passion was of giant proportions. He was born in Lagos, Nigeria with a Yoruba accent which seemed to give him more intensity. He was standing next to his car in the driveway with his FBI jacket plus other identifications. His junior was standing on the other side of the car as they were surrounded by the police.

"Drop to the ground, NOW!" Shouted the policeman holding the gun on Sunday.

Sunday, without moving, asserted, "I am FBI Field Commander Sunday. This is a national security issue. You need to move up the street till my team is done."

After more yelling with Sunday not obeying, there became a stalemate of sorts. Then four more cars came containing FBI agents. Some cars had two or three, or four agents, all reporting to Sunday. By this point, the police in command called off the hostage and sniper teams, resigning themselves that they would get control after the FBI was done.

Sunday went to the front door, which was open, and stated loudly, "I am Sunday and am here to help you. I am coming in, don't shoot!" There was no reply as Sunday slowly entered the home. Once in the foyer, his attention went to the formal living room. There he saw four dead men and Brand sitting on a chair just about in the center of them. Two of the men were savagely ripped apart, with their internal organs spread around the room. It was a grotesque sight, which Sunday will never forget. After viewing it, Sunday needed a few minutes to regain his composure.

Sunday then moved to Brand and squatted as he said, "My name is Sunday. Are you hurt? I am here to help. I am with the FBI, my people will clean this up, and we are going to get you out of here by the shuffle technique. Do you understand what I am saying?"

Brand, after a pause that felt like forever, slowly responded, "Not hurt, I understand," then after a moment, "Thanks."

Sunday now rushed to the front door, issuing out orders to the eleven people he commanded. Some were there to get the dead bodies out, while others were there to clean Brand up. They re-clothed him in their uniform with all the insignias. As the bodies of the dead were being bagged up and more agents were arriving, some of the original agents were leaving. In one group, there were three that left in one car. In the next group, there were two agents leaving in a different car. Agents were coming and going until the last group left with the body bags.

Sunday now informed the police that they were done with the scene and they could perform whatever they desired. He told them the entire home was searched and they found no suspect within the home. With that, he left as the last group of FBI agents left.

That was the way Sunday was, first to enter and last to leave. Sunday had an admiration for people like Brand, who work in the field mostly on their own. He always had a team of resources, but Brand, to him, was a one-man army. He was happy to get his job done. This was even better. He was proud to help a man like Brand.

As the young FBI agent drove Brand home, there were no words spoken until they were fairly close to Brand's rig.

The agent said, "It's been an honor, sir."

Now Brand seemed to come alive and, with a touch of scorn, said, "Why would you say that?"

The agent was now flustered and, after a moment, stated, "I meant no disrespect, sir."

Brand responded, "I killed two men, and my target got away. There is no honor here today."

No other words were spoken as Brand left the car and entered his rig. First, he called and checked on Bubba and told him they would regroup tomorrow. Then after taking care of Sweetbull, who could sense something was amiss and was on her best behavior.

Colonel Bolt was pleased with himself. The call to his friend in the FBI worked out well. There was something in the back of his mind that was bothering him. He knew that Subject 9 knew his name. That happened just before Darrell got killed last year. The problem being was he now being manipulated without his knowledge in helping Subject 9. That was always the fear in letting the subjects know too much. Even their sub-conscious mind can affect others. Bolt still was happy about the outcome, even if it might be bittersweet.

Chapter 12

OUT OF CIGARETTES

As if tonight did not go bad enough, Brand was now out of cigarettes and if he ever needed one, tonight was that night. So he jumped on Matilda and headed to the closest gas station. Where Brand lived, it was about fifteen miles before you hit any establishments. Before that just fields, some with animals grazing, others trying to grow things, and the rest just empty.

The night was bright with the full moon's illumination.

Everyone was monitoring Brand's position. There was Nina Woodhall waiting for Brand to draw out Dragonfly so she could be eliminated. Also, Big Bill had put a tracker on Brand's bike, waiting for the right time to strike. There was Dragonfly, who seemed to be able to locate Brand when she wanted to. Of course, there was Colonial Bolt, who always monitored his movements.

So as he drove down the lonely, empty road, feeling he was invisible, the exact opposite was true. After only five miles down the road, a police car's lights started to flash behind Matilda. If he ever wanted a cigarette, it was now. This would definitely put a delay to that.

Usually, Brand and the police would get along fairly well. To-night would be different in many ways. Brand could tell by the way the young officer approached him as he sat on his bike.

"Get off the bike now!"

Brand was taken aback but tried to act like all was normal. He already believed these were imposters. In his younger days, he may have tried a move to escape. Now he would play along. He truly did not want any more blood on his hands. And they may be real cops, he still was not sure.

"Yes, sir, officer. You seem angry. What's the problem?"

The young man now shouted his next commands.

"Turn around! Hands behind your back."

Brand complied, and he was handcuffed, standing next to his bike in the light of the police car's headlights. That is when Big Bill stepped out of the fake police car. He had such a smile. Even for an evil man, he had a warm smile. He was in no rush as he slowly strolled next to his young apprentice.

Big Bill began, "Well, if it isn't Mr. Wright, I told you we would meet again, and you were also right that this will be our last meeting." With that, he pulled out his gun and was just about ready to shoot Brand.

"Mr. Bill, you won, but I would like to have one last smoke. Do either of you smoke?"

Now Big Bill broke out laughing, "Is that all you have to say? You want a smoke? After that last speech, I expected so much more. So much better than can I have one last smoke!" With that, he seemed not to be able to control himself. Like when you can't stop laughing or giggling as it takes over your entire body.

Big Bill continued, "You know smoking will kill you!" With that, his laughter was doubling over. Even the young killer started to laugh, and then to finish it out, so was Brand. There were the three men, two holding guns and the third facing the bullets to come, and all were laughing. It was quite a peculiar sight to see.

Nina Woodhall received the phone call and immediately called General Stone.

"Hello, General Stone. How long for your planes to get to the target?" She provided the latitude and longitude of where Brand was located. The General was from the South and had a slight accent as he replied.

"That would be about five to six minutes. Our birds are in the sky."

Nina responded, "I want you to use double the power we had previously discussed."

"Well, Miss Woodhall, that would leave a pretty big hole. Are you sure that is what you want?"

"Do it! I will wait on the line!"

Then out of the blue, a woman's voice ended the laughter and brought everyone to her attention.

"Hello Gentlemen, I was hoping to be able to kill Brand Wright myself, and it looks like you're going to take that pleasure away from me."

Before anyone else spoke, Brand smiled and said, "I'd rather be killed by the pretty lady."

Now Big Bill was not amused. He said menacingly to Dragonfly, "Lady prepare to die."

As he spoke that Dragonfly kept moving closer to him and his partner. She had now passed Brand and was halfway between him and Big Bill.

It seemed like Big Bill was just about to kill her when a sound brought Brand to the ground. It started in the eardrums but seemed to go straight to the brain with a pain that was all in-compassing. It made it so no thoughts could be had. That pain was so great that soon he would lose consciousness.

As fast as the onset of pain started, it was over, except the situation was now reversed. Dragonfly had already killed the young fake officer. She then came over and unlocked Brand's handcuffs, and helped him up from the ground. It was Joy, but he knew she must be some sort of agent. He had that sense at the funeral. The big question is always, who is she working for?

Big Bill was laid down on the ground. Lying there without moving a muscle. It was uncanny to see him so vulnerable, yet there he was.

Dragonfly now was like a schoolgirl who had just got her first kiss from her Prince Charming. She was so happy with herself and looked at Brand, stating.

"I used a poison on him that paralyzed his body. He can still hear and see and most definitely feel pain. Unlucky for us, he won't be able to scream." And that part was said with a bit of sadness.

Brand ignored what she had said and bent down, looking closely into Big Bill's face.

"I told you to let it go. I warned you, death follows me."

Big Bill could say nothing. Sometimes, that is how it goes. One moment you have everything in control, and then, the situation reverses. It usually happens so fast and is so un-expected, but with hindsight could have been prevented if he had started to shoot her before she used that sound weapon, or if he had shot Brand quicker.

Now he was lying on the street, paralyzed and hoping for a quick death. Deep down, he knew he should have let it go. That this man, Brand, was luckier than any man had a right to be. Now he would die. The only question remaining was how?

Brand and Dragonfly were arguing on that exact issue. Brand having no real problem with him, was on the side of a quick kill. Dragonfly, who seemed more in charge, was enjoying his demise too much and wanted it to last much longer.

Chapter 13

MORE PROBLEMS

Brand and Chameleon had a formal system for when they wanted to communicate with each other. During one of their many talks, Brand explained that he did not want to use Chameleon to get out of life-and-death situations. Believing it would make him arrogant and sloppy. When he was in Gaylord's home, there was no thought of having Chameleon's help, just as when Big Bill had him handcuffed and ready for execution.

Now Chameleon had abruptly interjected, and time completely stopped in a circle of half a mile, with the group being in the center of that area.

Chameleon started the communication, which was strictly between Brand and Chameleon by mental telepathy. It went as follows.

"I am sorry to interject myself in your life, but your death is 17 seconds away. I know how you wanted to die a warrior's death. Being blown apart by a missile felt wrong. I feel you would be unhappy with your big event."

Even though time had been frozen within an area that Brand and company were in, there seemed to be a sense of urgency within Brand's mind. After a full minute of just thinking about what Chameleon had projected in his head, logic started to kick in, and a plan was formed.

Everyone else was frozen, including Dragonfly. Brand checked Dragonfly pockets looking for something. Then Brand opened his wallet, removing his driver's license and Visa card, even though he would not be using them. He then dropped his phone on the pile, which was an arm's length away from Big Bill.

Moving over to Matilda, he seemed to whisper something no one would know. Looking at the direction Dragonfly had shown up from, he went in that direction. After some running, he saw what was needed. Dragonfly's car, which he used the keys taken from her and drove to the scene of the confrontation.

Now he moved Dragonfly into the car's passenger seat and headed in the direction away from his home. Brand mentally told Chameleon to release time, yet he still was not far away enough, so Chameleon waited, knowing when they would be far enough away from the blast.

And what a blast it was. Even being miles away, the car felt the shock waves. One moment it was night, and the next such bright daylight you could not see. The firepower used was obscene. Who knows how many things died in that blast? Even in Brand's long life, he had never been that close to that type of explosion.

Questions always arise when situations become strange. And there was plenty of strange that had happened. The first priority was to get Dragonfly up to speed and stay under the radar.

After the blast, Brand pulled the car to the side of the road and switched seats with Dragonfly. They both had many questions and agreed it would be best to discuss the issues at her place.

Dragonfly's home was an abandoned building from the outside, but in one corner of the second floor, it was completely redone and looked like most beautiful modern rooms. It was one big room that used the two walls from the outside with created walls on the inside to create a large rectangle. Everything was in the one room in the open except for the bathroom. It was a marvelous use of colors and shapes to create a very comfortable, relaxing room with no obstructions to any of its main functions.

There was a very ornate French loveseat that Brand and Dragonfly sat together on. They agreed on each getting their questions answered by taking turns.

Dragonfly started with, "What just happened back there? How did I end up in my passenger's seat?"

"It's a long story, but I will give you the cliff notes and fill in after a few of my own questions. There is an entity that resides with me who informed me that a missile was going to strike us in 17 seconds."

Dragonfly looking like that is not nearly enough said, "Please explain in more detail, and then you can get your question."

Brand continued, "When Chameleon, that is what I call the entity, informed me of the missile, he can also slow down or freeze time within distinct areas. At that point, you were frozen in time, and I started thinking, why would they shoot a missile at us? Big Bill, his associate, and I were just collateral damage. It must have been you they wanted. So I decided to save you by putting you in your car and driving far enough away before releasing time. Once that happened, you became aware, and we were in the car."

Brand added, "I did leave my wallet, phone, and bike there, so they will think they killed all of us. That should give us some time to resolve this issue."

Brand continued, "I think I have earned my first question, "Who are you? Why do they want to kill you and how do you connect to me?"

Dragonfly who looked amused, "Well, in my world that is three questions. You did save my life, so here are your answers in reverse order. You don't remember me. We met almost two decades ago."

Brand now focusing strongly on her face, but really nothing was coming to mind.

Dragonfly continued, "You encouraged me to go to a facility that would help me, and all they did was put me in a high-security private prison. They call me Dragonfly, I don't really know if I ever had a real name. I am a hybrid and like to kill humans."

Brand now feeling a bit insecure, "So why did you not kill me?"

"You're a hybrid too, silly. You don't know that?"

Brand really looking confused, said, "I don't understand what you mean. How am I a hybrid?"

Dragonfly having that, you seriously don't know look answered, "I was created by humans, but you were mixed by them." As she said that, she pointed up to the sky. She continued, "You're part of the RB program- "

Now Brand interrupted, "What is that?"

"Reality Benders, people who can modify physics and break the realities that we associate with this plane of existence." She said it like it was common knowledge. "Heck you're more hybrid than I am with your Chameleon attachment."

Now Brand's brain was started to get a clearer picture, but there were still holes. Brand kept asking questions, "So why do they want to kill you so bad? Lots of people kill humans. They don't shoot missiles at them. What is so special about you?"

Dragonfly, for the first time, looked serious and replied, "They don't have an IQ test hard enough for me. Between my great intelligence and above-average reflexes plus my good looks and personality, they are scared of what I might do."

Then she added with a smile, "Now, please don't take this on how it is going to sound, but you are the greatest useful idiot I have ever met. I would never hurt you. That is why I intervened when Big Bill was attacking you. We are very much the same, whether called hybrids or freaks, all just words for different. Thank you for saving my life."

And with that, she open her arms, waiting for Brand to go in for a hug. There is something special about hugging. A surrendering of space and accepting of contact. Where you don't see the person's face but only feel their heart, their heat, or coldness. It is a sharing and expressing what no words can say. It was a great hug, and Brand later would say he had no idea how long it lasted. It felt like a moment, but a moment that went on past the counting of time. It was a long hug from two people who each had tremendous loneliness.

They agreed it was late, and after sleep, they would formulate a plan of action. Brand initially proposed he would sleep on the couch. But Dragonfly can be very persuasive, pointing out that it was a king-size bed of great quality. Meaning he had never slept on a bed like it. She promised not to hurt him with a smile and giggle.

For someone so intelligent, she also seemed very childish in attitude. It was a nice contrast to people who try to act smart and so serious.

Truth was it was a great bed, and in less than ten seconds, Brand was sound asleep.

Sam Smith was not happy, even though logic would determine he should be. Yet there are always loose ends. And in this case, it involved time. After reading the report, he decided he wanted a face-to-face with General Stone. Nina Woodhall was working with him on this operation, yet it felt like things were left out of the report.

Maybe it was just a mix-up in the time clock stamping sequence, just a mistake. That would seem like the most logical answer. He was probably just wasting his time. Because of the size of the blast, it will take days to sort it out, maybe even longer. Yes, he would definitely question the General. He texted Nina to make it happen today.

Gaylord didn't know who he killed and really couldn't care. He was now on the run, fearing going back to his home. Not knowing when or if he would be exposed, paranoia encompassed him. He had expected that team of mercenaries to rescue him. He contacted them right after receiving Brand's call. He had helped their leader with a certain land acquisition and was promised if he ever needed their services to just call. Once he saw that within the first second, his inquisitor had killed two men, his fear won over, that with the coming of night brought on his transformation.

After awakening in a field covered with blood, he came up with a plan. He had a friend, well, someone he had lent money to. His friend had said if he ever needed a favor, today was that day. It was an apartment complex. He rented a room from his friend with a fake name attached to it and settled in to wait and see if he would be exposed.

Brand awoke feeling refreshed and relaxed until the reality hit him of all the problems awaiting him. Gaylord was still alive and needed to be dealt with. Sweetbull would need to be attended to without giving away that he is still alive. And on that front, he needed to come up with a plan to resolve the Dragonfly dilemma. And there was the loss of Matilda, for which he still felt like he left a companion behind. Last but not least, he did not have a phone.

First on his list was to figure out a plan regarding Dragonfly's freedom. Even though she was not in their prison, she was still a prisoner. Now with all the new information, he was processing, he felt like a kindred spirit to Dragonfly and was determined to help her.

Chapter 14

GENERAL STONE

Even Generals were a bit nervous when dealing with Sam Smith. General Stone was not in that group and acted in his normal manner.

Sam started with, "Was something left out of the report?"

The General answered, "Usually," with a big smile that was not returned.

Sam was not amused with the General candor and continued.

"Why did you use so much explosive?"

General Stone looked like he did not want to get anyone in trouble since Nina Woodhall was in the room. "Well, I was under the assumption that collateral damage was not a factor and ultimate success of the mission was primary," then as an afterthought, "Just making sure," With the same big smile as before.

Sam Smith was not a man to be played with. The first questions were not important to him; the next was the reason he was called in for the meeting.

"The plane was in position at 10:13, yet the target was eliminated at 10:17. Why!?"

Now the General looked troubled, "Well, sir, it actually was 3:52 seconds later than it should have been. During that time, the plane was static on radar and non-communicative. We are researching it."

Sam looked sternly, "And that wasn't put into the report?"

The General now had his head looking down at the floor.

Before he could answer, Sam commanded, "You're dismissed."

After the General left, he looked at Nina and said, "This is not concluded until I get positive proof of Dragonfly death."

She responded with, "I will double the retrieval efforts, sir."

Bubba tried to get in touch with Brand, but he was not answering his phone. So the next morning, he went to Brand's rig only to find out Brand was not there. After hearing Sweetbull barking, knowing something was going on outside, Bubba used the key Brand had given him and gave her freedom. She was extra affectionate to Bubba and needed to be outside.

Once Bubba entered the rig, he could tell Brand had not been back since last night. There was no talk about Gaylord on the news, but the explosion near Brand rig was the talk of the town. Bubba's gut feeling was Brand was somehow involved in that event. No real information was being released, and the talk was it was a meteorite. Once it hit the ground, it landed on something that exploded. It was all very short on details and large on speculations.

Bubba decided to take Sweetbull home with him and locked up Brand's place, trying to be patience in hearing from his friend and thinking the best.

Chapter 15

COLONEL BOLT

Dragonfly was so many things, smart, of course, but sweet and so beautiful. She had made breakfast for Brand and herself. It consisted of a medley of fruits with exotic seafood containing Octopus and caviar and finishing with a chocolate desert.

It was amazing how nice she was to Brand, which only solidified his commitment to make things right. He now remembered her and had thought he was helping a troubled child. The reality was he was leading her to her prison. Yes, she had killed humans, yet looking at how they had treated her, what would they expect her to be, great-full?

Brand thanked her profusely for the meal but now had more questions.

He began with, "Dragonfly, do you know who Bolt is?"

She looked so pretty and replied, "He is your handler, your boss. He oversees the RB project. He has been monitoring you for years." She seemed surprised at how little Brand knew about the people around him.

Brand continued, "I have a plan to get your freedom. You will have to trust me. I need to talk to Bolt first to set it up. Will you trust me?"

She now looked him in his eyes, "Before last night, never! Now you are a different man, yes I will trust you, but I need to know your entire plan, every detail agreed?"

Brand, without hesitation, said, "Yes." Then he started to outline his plan in every detail to his new partner.

Colonel Bolt's worst nightmare was just about to be realized. He was in his office feeling sad about the lost of Subject 9. Wondering if any major developments would come from its outcome. Lost in thought, the phone in his office sounded like an air strike alarm. It jarred him before he picked it up, seeing it came from the lobby downstairs.

Answering with "Yes."

The receptionist responded, "Sir, Brand Wright is insisting on having a meeting with you right now. Should I have him removed?"

There was no answer, just silence on the other end.

"Sir, what would you like done?"

Bolt had dreamed of this nightmare, being face to face with Subject 9 and, even worse Subject 9 knowing how they are connected. He could avoid him, but obviously, Subject 9 had something important to communicate. His thoughts then went to Dragonfly, and he knew he would have to see him."

"Send him to my office. Thank you."

The two old men sat both in surveillance of each other. To say there was tension was definitely an understatement.

Brand broke the tension, "I have Dragonfly and I want to make a deal, but it has to be done my way. I have outlined when, where, and how it will proceed. The last page is what I want for making this all happen. And I have to say dropping a bomb on me does not make me happy. I will be in contact with you tomorrow after you have reviewed my plan. Make no mistake that I do not trust you, and if there are any deviations in my directions-this is not a threat, but what Sam Smith is worried about will definitely happen. Just follow the plan, and your interests will be served."

Bolt looking over the packet of pages, responded, "It will be done. Of course, I have to contact Mr. Smith for his approval. For the record, I had nothing to do with the missile attack. In regards to what you want, I can take care of that for you-

Brand interrupted, "It's personal. I will take care of it. Just provide the information."

Bolt looking troubled, "I like your plan, and I am sure Mr. Smith will too, but it relies all on you. We can't afford anything bad happening to you, so I will have two men accompany you for your protection."

Brand understood his position and accepted Bolt's offer.

Bolt responded, "Come back tomorrow, and we can complete your compensation and be ready for the big event on Friday, agreed?"

Brand replied, "Agreed."

And so the "big event," as it was now called, was happening in a few days.

Brand had found out so much information from Dragonfly, things about himself and people around him not seen. She had breached their computers as she laughed about how easy it was. Then she told him her story. Sam Smith was her nemesis. He had been involved in all aspects of her current existence, from her creation to her maximum security imprisonment ending with the attack on her life. Dragonfly did not just want to kill Sam Smith. She wanted him to feel terror with isolation and pain ending with hopelessness.

Death is such finality. Dragonfly's hatred for Sam Smith was greater than just the pleasure of removing a bad person from this plane of existence.

Brand knew the people he was currently dealing with would all double-cross him. It was in their nature, himself included in

that group. He had a plan as sure as Dragonfly and Sam Smith also had theirs. Whether Brand's plan or the others would work is not if but when they will double-cross each other and who then will be in control.

Brand was using Dragonfly's other car. She seemed to have so many possessions for her short time of freedom. Between her beautiful living conditions, the great food and bed, he wondered how well she would have done if left to her own accord. That is, with her not killing humans.

As he was driving to Bubba's home, knowing that Sweetbull really needed attention, his thoughts jumped around to all the different things within his head. The killing of the two men in Gaylord's home was troubling him. How many people did he just affect, and how worse will their lives all be? Cause and effect, with each action, we commit another effect that ripples down the time line effecting all around us.

Brand was determined in trying to save Dragonfly's life not just for one night but so she could actually enjoy what short time we all have. Maybe it was more for himself trying to find salvation for all his bad past acts, in the way Brand wants to kill Hector's killer. Trying to find redemption, unfortunately, in the wrong way.

When he arrived at Bubba's home, the greeting from Sweetbull was overwhelming. She literary knocked him over, licking his face. It reminded him how important they were to each other. He imagined if Sweetbull was lost and then found, how happy he would be. The greeting was over ten minutes long.

Bubba finally said, "Are you two getting a room?" With a big smile and laugh. They talked about many things but not Gaylord. It was like that subject was off-limits. Brand asked Bubba to take care of Sweetbull until Friday, when the big event will happen. Bubba readily agreed, and Brand left to go back to his rig to prepare for his payment in setting up the meeting between Sam Smith and Dragonfly.

That night Brand's thoughts were on Hector and Gaylord. They would forever be attached. If the public knew, he would also be attached to them. His thoughts were cold towards his enemies and himself. They say if you fight your enemy long enough, you become just like what you fight. He was supposed to be retired, enjoying the "Golden Years."

His mood turned cynical, seeing how so many poor people were struggling to keep their heads above water. Like most things in life, illusions, thinking about the golden years. Brand thinking it should be called the painful, broke lonely years. But who would look forward to that?

Chapter 16

KEEPING A PROMISE

The next morning by any rational person, was a beautiful Floridian day. Now, if you asked a person born in Florida, they may disagree, being the pickiest people when it comes to the weather. It was a day that just made you feel happy to be alive.

It was in direct contrast to what would happen latter in the day. Brand drove back to the office of Colonial Bolt. This time they were expecting him, and the receptionist had him take a seat until all were ready.

The wait was not long, and two men dressed in black with black face masks appeared. Brand was also wearing all black making them all look the same. The first man gave Brand a black face mask and they headed to the parking lot.

They all entered a black car with Brand getting into the back and the two government agents in the front. Once in the car, they handed Brand a box that contained a gun with a silencer and instructions to leave it when finished at the scene. After that, nothing was said during the ride to meet Gaylord.

They arrived at the apartment complex, which was typical Floridian style, with buildings forming a shape of a U with the pool in the center. Gaylord was staying on the first floor in a room near the office. The first man knocked on his door with three gentle knocks. After a moment, Gaylord spoke, saying, "Who there?"

The first man who seemed to do all the talking said, "I am detective Bill Tracey. We need to talk to you about the four men who died in your home."

"Let me see your badge," was Gaylord's reply.

The rooms all had peepholes on the door with a window next to the door. The two government men where standing by the door with Brand on the opposite side of the window. Even if Gaylord looked out the window, he would not see Brand.

People are trained to obey, so when Bill Tracey showed him a phony ID with a badge, Gaylord unlocked and unchained the door. As the door opened two inches, the first government man put his shoulder into the opening door, violently pushing it completely open.

Gaylord had fallen to the ground, and by the time he arose, all three men where now in the room. The second government man went to the door and stood guard. He also pulled the curtains completely shut and turned up the TV volume.

Now Detective Tracey told Gaylord to sit on the bed. There was a chair sitting on an angle towards it where Brand sat down.

Brand started by saying, "Relax, we never finished our conversation, now if you had known that Hector was my friend, you wouldn't have killed him, am I right?"

Gaylord stammering, "Yes, I never would have done that. I didn't know. Please, I have money. I will give you a million dollars in cash. It's at my home, please."

Brand already had his gun out with the silencer now attached.

"A million dollars, that's a lot of money." As Brand said that, he looked at Detective Tracey, who seemed like he was not listening.

Then Gaylord shouted, "I have 4 million in Bitcoin. You can have it all, please-"

Before the please had ended, Brand shot three rounds. Two rounds hit the left lung and the third the chest bone.

Brand responded, "Hector was worth so much more than that!"

The anti-climax was the ending to a sad situation. The three men went to their car and drove away. Nothing was said until they reached the parking lot from where they started.

Then the first man said, "See you on Friday." They parked, and Brand left.

The day was still so beautiful, yet Brand felt no pleasure. The feeling of knowing Hector's killer would never have another pleasurable day had a certain justice that seemed right. It was over with a much bigger problem looming. Hector was killed, and all Brand could do was avenge him. Dragonfly was still alive, and Brand had a chance to save her. That was all that mattered now.

Chapter 17

PLANS

Sam Smith had just ended the call with Colonel Bolt. It seemed like Brand Wright was going to bring Dragonfly in for containment a second time. How he has control over her to even get her to meet, let only give herself up, is almost too unbelievable. And that was the issue. Sam definitely did not trust Brand. And then there was Dragonfly, who was probably just using Brand to get to him.

Sam decided on a second plan in case whatever control or, more precisely, whatever plans Dragonfly has would be foiled. He called Nina into his office with instructions on this next stage of events. Also, to take some pleasure in her failure to kill Dragonfly. That was something he enjoyed doing, whether to Generals or his close associates, bask in their failures.

After Sam had briefed Nina on what had just transpired and what plans he had in mind to contain Dragonfly once the "meeting" was done. He would have it setup like rings on an onion. Each ring will have stronger security plus all the hardware and personnel needed. The only person in danger would be Sam Smith.

Nina, after hearing all that was said, began.

"Sir, can we speak off the record?"

Sam Smith looked at her intently, "Yes, you see a problem with my plans?"

Nina Woodhall had never critiqued her boss, yet smart leaders can handle hard truths. She began, "I have been studying Brand Wright's file, it's a huge file, and I ran some computer analysis, there is a pattern that emerges. You find the words like lucky, fortunate, fortuitous that riddle his missions-"

Lately, Sam's impatience could not be contained, especially in something as important to him as destroying Dragonfly, "What are you getting at? Get to it!"

Nina continued, "Look at his last mission with the Zombie problem, first, Darrell tried to kill him, and Joey shot Darrell. Then Joey and his associate had guns pointed at Brand ready to kill him-"

Sam, very much out of character, said, "He was lucky I sent that team in-" He stopped in mid-sentence, seemingly in shock with himself. He finally spoke, saying, "I get your point. That will be all." As Nina left the room, Sam told her, "Get Colonel Bolt in my office tomorrow."

If anyone was not intimidated by Sam Smith, it was Colonel Bolt. The two men sat alone in Sam's office, with Sam starting the conversation.

"You know Brand Wright more than anyone else. If you had to bet on who will win between Dragonfly, Brand Wright, or myself your answer is?"

Bolt, without hesitation, responded, "I would always bet on Subject 9. I don't like using his name, and it is never good for him to know our names."

Sam listened intently, "Why?"

Bolt replied, "He not only can change physics but also influence people. I have always worked on the policy of never mentioning his real name and never have him know my name. He could be influencing your decision-making without you even being aware of it.

Sam now asked, "Do you think I should go?"

Bolt again responded quickly, "No." Then Bolt added, "He always changes the deal he creates. He will double-cross you."

Sam thanked him for his input and had Bolt confirmed he would be there at the Big Event.

Then alone within his own thoughts, he felt challenged by Brand's meeting. That if he didn't show up, his ego would never let him live it down. Would he be afraid of Dragonfly and Brand Wright? He has great power and unlimited resources. And yet he was nervous. How can you tell what you're thinking is not your thoughts?

Sam called Nina into his office, "Off the record, do you think I should go?"

Nina hesitated, thinking this was a lose-lose question. She could see Sam wanted a true answer, so she said, "I would advise not to go."

Brand had given Bolt a very detailed plan on how the big event would proceed. He also made it abundantly clear that if anything happens before it occurs, it would spell disaster in a way they can't imagine. That they needed to follow the plan exactly, and their interests will be served.

He also made it crystal clear that if Sam Smith does not show up, then the worst will happen. If they send a fake, he will know. That all they need to do is follow the plan, he provided and trust him.

Now Brand also had told Dragonfly that if she trusted him, he would be able to gain her freedom from Sam Smith. She would be able to live a free life as long as she stopped killing. That included humans and hybrids.

She had agreed too quickly, and he knew that she would double-cross him. He also knew that getting a face-to-face meeting with her nemesis was something she could not resist.

Brand realized that once Sam Smith had Dragonfly in sight, he would not be satisfied until she was killed. This was just another opportunity to do that. He had no illusions that either one would betray him at the right moment.

The funny thing was this type of situation Brand was used to. Being in the field for years and knowing how things always change in the end, that was to be expected. Like when you are playing poker, and at the end, all is revealed. Sometimes the winning hand drops out, and the unexpected happens.

He was conditioned for these types of situations and, in a way, was looking more forward to it than Sam or Dragonfly. Whichever way this goes down if badly, it would be a warrior's death. And with his current situation, except for Bubba, Sweetbull, and his children, everyone else would be fine.

Deep down, after seeing so much death in his life and causing some of it, he was ready for the end. To him, his final breath would start his big event. At a certain age, life becomes routine and weary. So many you loved have gone, and all that is left is you standing on an empty battlefield.

Chapter 18

THE BIG EVENT

To most people, Friday is a special day, the start of the weekend. Yet to a small group of people, Friday was much more than that. It would direct their future courses in life, a day of destiny.

The day was Thursday, and the weather was very non-typical for Florida, having a light grey sky with gusty winds and a cold breeze. Many would say it was a horrible day. In reality it was just as Brand wanted it. It reflected the conditions within his soul, the eternal fight to be a good man. The overall grey that his soul felt. How many good acts make a bad act ok?

The wind reflected his constant turmoil within himself. There was an Indian expression just before the battle, "Today is a good day to die!" That is how he felt. And the cold breeze was the way mankind treats mankind. Cold shows the trickery and deceit that is so prevalent.

Dragonfly's plans involved a special type of net plus smoke and a jet pack. If it works, she will be able to kidnap Sam Smith and then destroy him in her specially planned ways. Laughing to herself thinking, Brand could think he would broker a peace deal. He clearly doesn't understand the hatred she has for her enemy. When it came to people like Sam Smith and herself, there was only room for one to prevail. Each knowing the other could destroy them, it becomes natural that if brought together, only one will walk away.

She had some other surprises waiting, and all was set. Like a schoolgirl going to her first prom and knowing she will be prom queen, this will be one of her greatest victories, and she will not forget that Brand made it possible.

Sam Smith had the latest weapons, both defensive and offensive, plus a small army to protect him and destroy Dragonfly. From sharpshooters to tanks that looked like trucks. There was the initial circle that could destroy everything within that circle with a 100% kill rate. Of course, he would be out of that circle when it happens. But there were more soldiers around the second and third circles. He was assured even Houdini could not escape.

Brand knew a lot of people. He had a friend that owned 40 acres of land that was empty and perfect for his planned meeting. After a little small talk, his friend gladly let him use it for the day but only if he could be there. Brand tried to warn him it might be dangerous, but that was the requirement if he wanted to use the land.

Bubba and Brand prepared the land with flags denoting the two sides and a line for each not to cross. It looked a lot like the old football stadiums that just had seats on each side but not in the end zones. It was hard work, but once finished would make it easier for all who followed.

In the center between the two lines, which were there for no one to cross, was a rectangular table with three chairs. The table was aligned North with a chair on the West, East, and South points.

One for each of the players, their armies will be on their sides behind the line. Except for the South player, he has no army and only one person waiting for him.

Sam Smith called Nina Woodhall into his office. He wanted to change the plans that were agreed on for The Big Event.

He began with, "Nina, I want to add something to The Big Event, but I do not want you to have any formal or informal contact with Subject 9. Contact Bolt and have everything go through him."

Nina was caught off guard and just said what was in her mind, "Why are you now calling Brand Wright, Subject 9? And what is the big deal about being direct with him?"

Sam looked at her with feelings he rarely felt, like someone who has seen the light to one who still is in the dark.

"I have been reviewing his file very closely and have been in contact with Bolt. It is best that he never knows your name. His sub-couscous negative thoughts could harm you. It would be best if he never knew you fired a missile on him!"

Nina was speechless, his words slowly starting to sink in. She had proved she was a killer, and even though the kill never happened, she would now pay the consequences as if it did.

"I understand, sir. Thank you, sir. What do you want changed?"

Sam began, "I want two of my own men with me at the table for my security. It is that or no deal."

Bolt contacted Brand by text, saying that the plan needed to be modified. Sam Smith wants two men to accompany him at the table. Please confirm this text, thank you. When Brand received the text, he was in a bad mood. His response was quick and to the point.

Bolt received Brand's reply text, and it went as follows, "I will give you 15 minutes to get yourself and Sam Smith on a video call. Text me with the information to join. If that does not happen, I will consider the deal default, and Dragonfly and Sam can settle it on their own. I am warning you, not threatening that if that happens Sam's worst nightmare will come true."

Bolt was smiling inside. Deep down, he was proud of the way Subject 9 seemed to always be in control. Here he was, pushing a huge power around like he was directing children on a school bus. It has a beauty all to itself that so few could appreciate. Bolt knew he was one of the few.

He contacted Nina and explained the situation and that they only had 11 minutes to respond. Within 4 minutes of that it was confirmed that the call would take place, and with 4 minutes to spare, all three men were looking at each other.

Sam began with, "For my protection, two of my men will accompany me during our meeting."

Brand's mood was no better than when he received Bolt's text and responded.

"It seems like I should be the one to be worried. You did shoot a missile at me."

Sam quickly said, "For the record, I had nothing to do with that!"

Brand answered, "I believe that is partly correct, but it does not matter. Life is made of moments, special moments. When you watch a football game, the football moves up and down the field. Within the game, there are special moments, and in those moments, there can be one that defines the win, that great special moment. I am giving you the opportunity for that type of special moment. If you're too scared to be there, then you can fix your own problem. Use a big imagination, for your enemy has tremendous hate and plans that a normal person could never think of. If there are any deviations from my plans, then I will walk away, period. Now, are you coming to the table alone?"

Sam replied, "How can you trust Dragonfly? She would never willingly submit to containment again. She must be planning to double-cross you and me."

Brand, smiling, said, "I totally expect her to double-cross me, as I expect you to do the same. That is what makes that moment so special. Three people at a table all planning on double-crossing each other." Then he added, "With all your power and resources, Dragonfly was not scared to come to the table alone, so are you coming alone?"

Bolt, who had not spoken the entire time, was watching in amazement at how subtle Brands words were, like using scared just before asking the question. The whole speech was about a moment. He was baiting Sam and doing it with ease.

Sam, seemingly upset, responded, "I'll be there alone." Then his feed ended with just Bolt and Brand left on the call.

The two men did not speak, just staring intently at each other with their own thoughts. Bolt disconnected first.

The game of Poker has many unique elements. Like most games, it emulates life in certain aspects that get amplified and used in winning. Brand knew he was in a poker game, and the other players had stronger hands. It reminded him of the play "Fiddler on the Roof," being the precariousness of that act.

Chapter 19

SHOW TIME

Friday had finally arrived, with Dragonfly and Sam Smith ready to kill each other. The weather was awesome, with a beautiful blue sky and temperatures in the high 70 degrees capping it off with low humidity. Perfect for almost any activity or event. Fridays were always a special day in Brand's youth and today reminded him of that excitement in the past.

The cars and trucks started showing up at 11 am. All were going to the government side of the divide. And there were so many of them. Then the helicopters arrived with men and women dressed ready for combat. Sam Smith may be at the table alone, but he had an army 30 feet from him. Hundred were there, including medical personnel.

Dragonfly's team didn't show up until about 5 minutes before 12 pm. Only five trucks showed up. All identical color and style, having all her personnel wearing the same type and color jumpsuits.

Dragonfly was wearing the most unusual dress ever seen. It had two parts, with a body suit being one part with a negative charge. Then there was a second garment that had a positive charge which floated apart from the body suit about one to one and a half inches. Its design had a checker pattern with what appeared to be silver chains attached to a material that reflected the light creating multiple color patterns. As she walked to the table, it had a mesmerizing appearance with so many colors being displayed and the way the two materials never touched each other.

Sam Smith, who was still on his side of the line, slowly started walking past it when Dragonfly made her bold entrance. If she did have any fear, she did not show it, which made her stroll to the table more impressive. She arrived first, with Sam following while Brand was already standing by the southern chair.

Brand acted like a host, welcomed both, and asked them to be seated. They seemed to sit at the same time, with each watching the other's actions. Once they had seated, Brand seemed to become relaxed.

Brand open the meeting between the three of them.

"Now we can relax as there will be no distractions from either side. I have something to say to you both and want your full attention. Before I start, turn your heads to your respective groups and observe them carefully."

At that, Brand stopped speaking and turned to Sam and said, "Can you feel the stillness? It feels unnatural. We are outside of the world's time. That means hopefully we can all reach an agreement without being distracted by either side."

Then he looked at Dragonfly, knowing she had a complete understanding of what was happening.

Brand began again, "I have something to say to both of you, and now that I have your attention, I will begin. Imagine a three-way chess game. On the West side, we have Sam Smith, all-powerful with almost unlimited resources. And on the East, we have Dragonfly. Intelligence beyond measure, the kind that can change everything. Two very equal opponents, with either side being able to win on any given day. For these two great enemies to reach a draw is actually a win, even if it does not feel like it to either side."

Sam looked bored, and Dragonfly amused, neither taking his words seriously, which now annoyed Brand.

Brand continued, "Everything is composed of energy, frequency, and vibrations. Just as Nikola Tesla said, and each of us has an energy signature that is unique. Not only that, but within that signature, thoughts and feelings are all present in current time."

Now Brand saw that Dragonfly acted like she understood, but Sam looked confused, so he said it differently.

"Sam, if you think about killing Dragonfly, Chameleon will know. Chameleon can control his energy, frequency, and vibrations. That is what allows him eternal life and the ability to change form. Yet he can do so much more than that. Demons, vampires, jinns, werewolves, and even aliens all have something in common, human characteristics. Chameleon is more like a computer with curiosity.

To understand how Chameleon thinks is hard. Let me try to give you an example. There are a million ants for every person on the planet. We don't notice them till they bother us, and then we destroy as many as we can. We destroy the nest. Well, imagine instead of ants but planets. And life like us living on all of them.

Chameleon knows your energy signatures and can monitor them effortlessly. If either of you plan the demise of the other, then you both will be turned off. He can either put you into a brain-dead state or actually turn your energy off, meaning you will die. And if either of you tries hurting me, you will be turned off." At this point, he stopped to look closely at his audience.

Sam Smith now had something to say, "Your bluffing. We have been monitoring Chameleon for decades and have never seen those attributes you mention."

Brand, looking very serious for the first time, almost in a whisper said the following words.

"If you're right, then you win, but if you're wrong, hear me very clearly." And then, with a long pause, Brand said, "Nothing can save you."

The two men were staring eye to eye. It did not end until Sam said, "Continue, I am listening."

Brand continued, "The deal is simple, Sam. You will leave Dragonfly alone and not interfere in the rest of her life, while Dragonfly agrees not to kill anyone, human or hybrid. Also, she will leave you alone and not change the world too drastically too quickly. Now I know to you both that it feels like you're losing, but after time, you will see you're both winners. Except for the fact that you both were beaten by the third player, a useful idiot."

Brand now turned to Dragonfly to see her response.

Dragonfly looked at Sam and said, "Your lucky he is on your side!" Then she looked at Brand and said, "That is twice you have beaten me, nicely played," and she gave him the sweetest look he had received in a long time.

Yet there seemed to be more in that look. That is the thing with looks, they can say so much while still holding secrets.

Then Brand looked at Sam, who shook his head ever so slightly up and down, saying, "Deal."

Brand continued, "Just two more things. First, once I release time, you both need to call off whatever prior plans you had, or everything will be ruined, and you both will be dead. Here is the neat part, I want you both to shake hands and hold them until I say ok. To everyone watching, you both just sat down, performed a handshake, and left the table. It will be known as the 2-second meeting. Everyone will want to know what happened, but only the three of us will know."

With that, Brand was feeling really great, finally doing something good without having to inject bad to get there.

Sam Smith and Dragonfly performed the handshake, and just as they touched hands, Brand said, "Done," and with that, turned his back to both of them and started to walk South.

Maybe it was just luck or instinct that something bad was going to happen. Brand had turned around again to face Sam and Dragonfly. The area they were standing in was now becoming overwhelmed with smoke. It was multicolored, which seemed surprising at the time. Its effectiveness was powerful, and Brand knew he would only have seconds before all would be lost to sight.

That is when Dragonfly put her right hand to the back of her neck, manipulating some sort of control panel. With the next moment the outer dress violently moving towards Sam Smith. Within a second he was wrapped within it, the material had seemed to disappear with the chains in the criss-cross pattern locking together. Both Sam's arms were wrapped by the now chain restraints.

Then Dragonfly connected another chain to connect Sam's restraint to her like you would attach a dog to a leash. This all happened very quickly with the smoke coverage only seconds away from making Brand eyes blind to all that would happen next.

It was a feeling of motion that next caught Brand's sensations. By this time his brain knew both sides would be sweeping in but the right side seemed quicker.

One of Dragonfly's men was wearing a jet suit which had been outfitted with a metal harness. Dragonfly's plan was based on electromagnetism which is how the outer dress left her body and entangled Sam. Now her negative charged body suit was being attracted to the metal harness which was positively charged and within in a second they were attached.

By this point Brand could hear Sam's men getting close with only seconds to provide Sam's escape he made his decision.

Within another second the smoke would overtake everything while Dragonfly would escape with Sam dangling below her and her jet man.

Brand's gun was already out and with almost no sight available emptied his clip at only one target. Seven shots fired and which rounds saved the day will never be known. The next second Brand was on the ground hit with a Taser.

As he went to the ground so did Sam Smith. The chain attaching him to Dragonfly was broken by Brand's shots and gravity did the rest. He had about a four foot fall and was quickly attended to. Now there were teams of people, some blowing the smoke away while others were accessing all that had happen and if Dragonfly could be caught.

Her escape was below any radar could detect while her speed faster than the helicopters could attain. The attention then went to Brand and what should be done with him. Bubba was trying to get to the action but was being restrained by all the soldiers there.

Now Sam had regained his composure and was not hurt just shaken up. He commanded all around Brand with, "Let him go!" And then looking Brand directly in his eyes, "Thank you."

Brand had wanted there to be no violence, a peace based on a lie. Most times lies are bad yet if peace could be had on a bluff, that was Brand's dream. Two great powers afraid to attack based solely on a lie. To Brand that was beautiful poetry and it was so close to happening.

Eventually things were sorted out with Brand and Bubba being allowed to leave. Dragonfly only had herself and one accomplice which were able to get away. The other three vans were self driving vehicles being completely empty inside.

It seemed everyone but Brand were content. Dragonfly had her chance, even if it did not succeed it was fun trying. Sam Smith had faced his moment and in his own way had won. Being that close to Dragonfly she could have killed him quickly if that was her desire. He had passed his own test and that was good enough for him. Brand on the other hand felt like a complete looser.

Chapter 20

ANSWERS

Two weeks later, Sam called Nina into his office for her new assignment. To some, it may have looked like she failed. Failed to kill Dragonfly, yet she had proven herself. She had found Dragonfly, which itself is an accomplishment. And she would have killed her except for what would have been called in the old days, an act of God. The fact that Dragonfly lived was not her fault.

"Nina, you have done well and proven yourself in the Dragonfly affair. The problem we have in Antarctica regarding the Pyramid, I want Subject 9 to investigate and resolve the problem. It is vitally important that he is not deceived or forced to go. It has to be his own choice. Have Bolt give him the file, and if Subject 9 chooses to go, let me know."

Nina was in a bit of shock. It seemed like Sam Smith had changed after the Dragonfly meeting. He was nicer but more than that, maybe more caring. His communications were longer and more open. So she felt less hesitation in asking.

"Sir, regarding my future plans, are they still a possibility?"

Sam replied, "First we make you a Senator for name recognition and then President." Sam was smiling, which Nina had never seen him do. He said, "I was thinking Senator Woodhall from the Sunshine State of Florida."

Bubba had rented a boat for himself and Brand to just go sailing. No fishing or diving, just drinking and remembering Hector. With no cell phones, just a boat in the middle of the Gulf of Mexico, Brand told the complete tale of what happened at the meeting with Dragonfly and Sam Smith.

After the tale was told, Bubba asked, "So, you were bluffing?"

Brand replied with his devilish smile, "It sounded good!"

Bubba just looked at his friend in amazement.

PART 2

THE FIRST PEOPLE

Chapter 21

ANTARCTICA

Things tend to come full circle, so when Colonial Bolt arrived at Brand's rig, he returned the favor when Brand turned up at his office. Sweetbull was only into greeting the stranger with a wagging tail and many licks. So much for pit bulls being mean. Brand greeted him at the door and invited him in to discuss whatever was on his mind.

Six months ago, Bolt would never have visited Subject 9, yet so much had changed that the old fears had to be dismissed. Also, he wanted his request to be presented right and doing things yourself assures it will be done the way you want.

Bolt began, "Ahh, Mr. Wright.."

Brand interrupted, "Brand, please."

Bolt resumed, "Eh, Brand, I wanted you to look over this file," which he was holding in his left hand. Bolt continued, "We would like you to go there and look into the situation, but it is totally up to you. If you don't want to go, absolutely no problem. Everything we know is in the file, and it is very understandable if you don't want to go."

Brand, now smiling, said, "What a way to make me go. It reminds me of something I would do! I will read the file and let you know."

Bolt, now looking relieved, "Thank you, if you do decide to go, your mission compensation plus passport and everything else you will need will be provided. Please read the report carefully. You don't have to do this!"

Brand thanked him for his honesty. Why do people always think that honesty will never work? When all the facts are clearly shown, it eliminates so many other negative emotions. The file was not that big, and there were some flash drives included.

To some, the past is just that, something that is over and needs not be bothered with. Others, it is the roadmap from where we began to where we may be going. Brand was part of the others, as he liked studying many aspects of the past.

When studying history, it is more like always trying to figure out a puzzle. First thing is to forget the mainstream thoughts and look at all the fringe theories. One area of the past that shouts to our failure of knowledge is the Pyramids. This was an area that Brand had studied for decades. There were the usual questions and then the deeper questions.

Take, for example, the question of construction. Brand had researched the one ramp, two ramps, zig-zag up each side, zig-zag around the inside of the pyramid, water-powered ramps, and of course, the cement theory.

In looking at the Great Pyramid inside the King's chamber, the sarcophagus does not even sit in the center but is off to the right side. The walls are finely polished, but the floor looks haphazard and crude. With absolutely no markings of any kind on the walls or sarcophagus. So many questions with so many theories.

These structures demand our attention while beating even time itself. So as Brand began to look through the file Bolt had given him, it revealed an interesting story.

The Antarctic treaty regulates international relations with the continent. The thing is, there are no wars there, no traveling there except for scientific studies. It is agreed by the full international community and has been that way for more than 60 years.

Another strange thing that leads to more questions. Why can the entire world agree to this without some country disregarding it? What are they protecting? What are they afraid of? Yes, strange things generate lots of questions that are right to ask.

The report started with a bit of past history regarding the Antarctic. The real attention was on what was below the ice. There is a huge ice tunnel that goes for miles ending with a pyramid three times the size of the Great Pyramid in Egypt. This one is not made of stone and is quite different than any others on Earth.

It was made with a metallic substance that seemed to have a colorful shimmer to it. The ramp that led to the doorway, which met the ice tunnel, had a slight rise to it facilitating getting to the triangle door which led into the pyramid.

The problem being there is an energy field surrounding the entire structure. On the right side of the triangle, door was a triangle shape with a button inside of it. This was behind the energy field. Anything trying to activate the button gets destroyed by an electrical flash so intense that the entire object disintegrates. The location of the button was about seven feet high from the ramp's floor.

There were two flash drives that showed what happened when the button was tried to be pushed. As soon as something touched the energy field, it destroyed the entire object, not just the portion that entered the field.

Supposedly they had tried all different options, from sound waves to their own energy field. They tried to shoot through the field, but nothing worked. Everything that touched it was destroyed. The basic aspects of the mission were simple, gain access to the pyramid, do a fast reconnaissance and return hopefully alive.

In times like this, Brand was like Big Bill, knowing he should not involve himself in this operation. That only trouble can happen. Yet maybe it was his lifetime attraction to pyramids, maybe it was a death wish. Brand really could not tell, only that his inclination was to go and try.

Chapter 22

THE PYRAMID EXPERIMENT

Once in Brand's youth, for a science project he created an experiment involving a self-built pyramid. The test was to see if two tomatoes would age the same if one was in a pyramid and the other was just under a hat. Brand was careful in setting both tomatoes at the same height within the pyramid and hat, also, in aligning the pyramid on the compass points of North, West, East, and South.

Unfortunately, or maybe luckily, he forgot about the project, and when he finally reviewed the results, they were amazing. How long the experiment lasted until Brand finally reviewed it is undetermined. There was no denying what he saw after removing the hat which was covering the tomato. It was a mess, to put it plainly. It had rotten and semi-decomposed with juices and molded tomato skin forming a disgusting appearance.

The other tomato under the pyramid was quite different. It still had its form with having four singular strange cut lines equally spaced apart. These lines consisted of very small cut marks on an angle going from the top of where the line started to the bottom of where the line ended. Each cut mark was followed by another on the opposite side of the line but lower and then repeated again till it reach the bottom of the cut line.

It reminded Brand of the lines on a baseball which had similar qualities, except in this case, there were four cut lines with stitches making small slit marks following the opening on the tomato. The actual condition of the tomato was perfect, and it could be eaten without any problems.

At the time, Brand was young and had many other interesting things happening. Also, the thought of taking a picture never entered his mind. In those days taking pictures was not like today. First, you needed a camera and then film.

Even though no pictures were taken, Brand never forgot what he saw. Sadly he could not remember what materials he used in the pyramid's construction. He did remember that he set the tomato one third the height of the total space inside the pyramid.

When looking at the Great Pyramid, the King's chamber is not in the center but off to the side. The Queen's chamber is right in the center and was how he based his location for the tomato inside.

Bottom line was something special happened to that tomato, and it occurred with just a homemade pyramid causing it. From that day, Brand always had a longing to understand them better.

It seemed like now would be a perfect time to resume those studies, even if it meant his possible death.

Brand met Bubba to take care of Sweetbull while he was away. During their conversation, Bubba, of course, wanted to know where Brand was going. After all that had happened during the last year, Brand could care less about the top-secret nature of his mission. He told Bubba about all the details and even showed him the videos on the flash drives.

Bubba had definitely changed since he met Brand. Bubba always had a fascination for fringe elements. That fascination would take place from afar, like when he first hired Brand to film that haunted house. Being around certain people can really influence certain other people. Bubba no longer wanted to be an observer. This effect Bubba attributed to Brand persona.

Bubba thought to himself about when he went in to rescue Hector and Brand from the demon. Then there was the time he saved Brand from Gabriel Hand, a nasty vampire. And just recently, when they went to avenge Hector's killer Gaylord Fisher.

If Brand was going, he wanted to go along. Bubba wanted to experience the event first hand, and knowing Brand, he would need his help somewhere along the way.

Bubba asserted, "I want to go along. You will need my help!"

Brand, now having fun at his friend's expense, "Bubba, it is a restricted area. No one is allowed there except scientists." Looking at his friend with an expression of what can I do, Brand continued, "It's a top-secret mission. You need super high clearance, heck I should kill you right now for all the info you know." Brand having a big smile on his face. If that wasn't enough, he followed with, "Who's going to take care of Sweetbull?"

Looking at Bubba, Brand said, "If we can't go together, then neither of us will go. I suggest you get your warmest clothes 'cause I hear it is cold down there."

Bubba now smiling, asked, "How can you be so sure they will agree to us both going?"

Brand, with an evil smile, said, "Bubba, I have them in the palm of my hand, like putty. Trust me, they will agree."

In Poker, the art of winning is, at times, a lot to do with having a losing hand. So many times Brand has had to win with that losing hand. Brand thought to himself, this time it is different, Bolt's people are desperate, and I can make demands.

And that is what Brand was doing, writing down all the requirements for his participation to do the mission.

Bubba and himself would be compensated on a daily rate, including paid transport costs plus any other fees that may occur. Also, a complete set of clothing suited for the environment for both men. All medical expenses are to be covered for any injuries that happened during the mission. As he prepared the list of demands figuring there would be negotiations, he added things that he assumed would be rejected and could use them as a compromise for other more important items.

Brand visited Colonel Bolt to go over his requests and confirm whether they were agreed upon. Once that is settled positively, Bubba and himself would do the mission. In Brand's mind, he will make sure that Bubba is not near anything that will kill him. He also knew that Bubba would love the experience of going there, especially the way the military would do it.

The two men, Brand and Bolt, had a strange relationship. Neither trusted the other, with both having high respect for each. Brand submitted his requests, with the first being that Bubba will be accompanying him on the mission.

Bolt seeing that started, "You understand that your friend does not have the clearance or training needed, and you would be putting his life at risk."

Brand responded, "It is his decision, and I will not go without his company."

Bolt knew that it was almost a death sentence going there. He also knew that Sam Smith really wanted Subject 9 to go but only by his own decision. If he denied the request, it would all be over with Subject 9 walking away. Whatever Bubba would see if he didn't die there when he returned, no one would believe him. Then his thoughts went to if he denied the request, maybe he is saving both Subject 9 and Bubba.

Most people never really have another person's life in their hands. Their decisions aren't the factor in whether that person will see another day or not. Men at war in command know that feeling. Bolt had made that decision many times, and it is never easy.

Bolt agreed to Subject 9 requests cause, in the end, it was the most logical thing to do. He will satisfy Sam Smith plus maybe Subject 9 will be able to enter the pyramid. The fact that Subject 9 wants to go also played into his decision. The worst scenario is Subject 9 will die, and quite frankly, he is old and will die soon anyway.

Brand was surprised that all his requests were granted. It conveyed to him how badly they needed him to resolve this problem. The only thing left was when they would leave, as there were things that needed to be addressed, like Sweetbull's care and plans if they never return.

When Bubba heard the news, you would have thought he was winning the lottery. Like a kid who wanted to space travel and now knows he is going to the moon. It made Brand feel extremely pleased with himself to know he had brought his friend so much happiness.

In reality, Bubba would be in for some rude awakenings about how military missions really worked. Yet that is half the fun, finding out how things really are. With all of Bubba's joy Brand reminded him to make sure all his last wishes were written down. Anytime one goes on a mission like this, you never can be sure you will be returning home. Writing down your last wishes and goodbyes is greatly appreciated by all who are left when you don't return.

In Brand's case, he had one chance to succeed, and if his hunch was wrong, all would be lost.

Chapter 23

IT BEGINS

Bolt contacted Nina Woodhall with the pertinent information. She thanked him and then contacted her boss Sam Smith relaying the news. Sam seemed different after his meeting with Brand and Dragonfly.

In ways, he was kinder or more caring about the immediate people around him. Yet it was more than that, something hard to define. Some call it a gut feeling. Other call it vibes. Whatever name you may use, he seemed to have changed.

Nina told Sam, "He accepted the mission willingly with some conditions." Now she was waiting for him to inquire about them, the way her "old Sam" would ask.

Sam seemed satisfied, "Good. Dismissed."

Whatever Bubba was expecting, the reality was very different, yet he seemed so happy about it all. It reminded Brand of his father and when he brought Brand to help him at work one day. Long hours and hard work, but it was great.

Bubba looked at Brand and asked, "So are we going first class? How long you figure it will take to get there?"

Brand was all smiles. Lately, all his anger seemed to have been released killing Hector's killer and that he tried to broker a peace treaty with Sam and Dragonfly.

"Well, it will definitely not be first class. Probably a cargo plane, and we will be in the back. As for how long, figure longer than seems right." And with that Brand chuckled to himself, looking like he was reliving old memories. Even Brand was surprised at how they eventually arrived at Antarctic.

Major Lee was Bubba and Brand's liaison for the mission. The other team members will be at the site waiting, as Major Lee had stated. He was all business with very little personality, at least that is what he was portraying. He stayed unusually close to Brand, never being more than three feet from his side.

Bubba was in awe of the way the military worked. Brand and Bubba were fitted with state-of-the-art winter wear. That consisted of boots and socks, underwear, pants, and jacket. Then there were the two different types of gloves worn together with a hat. It did not end there. They had augmented-reality goggles that were downloaded with pertinent information that may be needed for the mission.

And, of course, the backpack loaded with the necessities of life plus much more. Make no mistake, the USA has the greatest military currently in the world. Most times, the public gets just tiny little peaks of what is really out there. For that matter, how the world really works.

Brand did not trust Major Lee, period. Knowing you're being shadowed just makes it worse. There is only so much you can control, and then you just have to let it be.

After getting all the preparations done, they headed out to the military base to get their plane. Sure enough, it was a cargo plane with straps in the back and a bench. No window seats or first class available.

Bubba looking at Brand, said, "How did you know?"

Brand replied quietly, even though it was loud in their area, "No record of the trip. As far as the world is concerned, this never happened." And then, smiling, said to Bubba, "Welcome to being a spy! They always have plausible deniability if things go bad."

The ride was long, and Bubba was very happy he had taken many snacks and plenty of water, as Brand had suggested when they were planning things. Even in uncomfortable spots, eventually, you settle down and can fall asleep. Bubba was awake most of the time, while Major Lee and Brand seemed to fall asleep with little issues.

They landed on some island which no one knew the name or if someone did, they were not saying. After leaving the plane, they went to what seemed to be the only building there. After refreshing themselves and having a meal, they went to the beach and waited for the fishing boat.

It was a large boat and could easily be classified as a ship. In contrast to its size, the crew were few and rarely seen. Captain Saul was an old man who seemed wiser than even all his years. He is the kind of person that always seems to know more than he reveals. There seemed to be an instant friendship between him and Brand, which allowed Brand some space from Major Lee.

Captain Saul and Brand would go into the Captain's room to play chess. The Captain's room was off-limits to everyone, so when Major Lee tried to enter, he was denied with no uncertain words.

As Brand entered the room, Captain Saul was behind him. Major Lee was following the Captain and was third in line. Once the Captain entered his cabin, he turned around quickly and stated. "This room is off limits to you Major Lee." It was said with the type of authenticity that only a ship Captain has. It is well known that a Captain is King on his ship. His words are the law, and to break that law is very dangerous to any who tries.

The Major was startled by the forcefulness in the Captain's voice. He realized that he could force the issue by being a higher rank. Major Lee was very pragmatic. His orders were to stay with Brand for the entire mission, reporting on any unusual happenings. To penetrate the pyramid and report back with what was found. They were on a ship and Brand had no intention of escaping. There would be no point in upsetting the Captain for something with such little gain. He would suspend his orders till they reached Antarctica. After that, he would be Brand's shadow while completing his mission.

Once in the Captain's cabin Brand spoke first, "Thank you for that!"

The Captain gave a wide grin and shook his head from side to side. They played chess with a chess clock set for 10 minutes. They were both fast players, never needing the full 20 minutes. The Captain was a bit better, but when one would make a critical mistake, the other would pounce on it.

Some players will toy with the win, dragging it out as a cat plays with a mouse before the eventually kill. You can learn a lot about someone by the way they play chess, win or lose. Both Brand and Captain Saul were direct when it mattered.

Captain Saul said, "It's a dangerous mission, sure you know that and have your reasons. We will hit the mark in two days and then wait till the rendezvous. She's a beauty!" It was clear Captain Saul was much more than just a Captain. Brand had dealt with people like him in the past. Mysterious people who always knew more than they should and just pop in and out of events.

Brand inquired, but the Captain was not telling, which deep down was fine for Brand. Surprises keep people young and if they are good surprises, are wonderful moments in one's life.

The next two days were uneventful, with the Captain and Brand playing a lot of chess. The meals were delicious as the cook was proud of his work and put his love into it. It was a very peaceful two days which seemed to pass quickly.

Major Lee seemed to relax compared to his usual focus. Bubba still had great excitement about what was to come. On the third day, it happened.

They were all on the deck, Bubba, Brand and Major Lee with Captain Saul, as the waters started to disappear. She rose from the water like a wall of metal being so huge that the total horizon was blocked out. Captain Soul's ship became tiny when compared to the sight being seen. As the waters washed away from her, she was magnificent. A beauty of science and technology that transcended into art. A picture of what people can achieve that individually would be impossible.

They were looking at one of America's top-secret nuclear submarines. The thing about America is that most nations make or buy their arms and then brag to their enemies and the world about what they have and how strong they are.

America does not do that. It hides its best weapons, always wanting to surprise its enemies. Most will never see the incredibly impressive technology that America has. Not to mention what new things are always in development.

It was much wider than what is seen in the movies. After boarding a motorboat, they met the target. They had to climb a rope ladder which Bubba and Major Lee did with much more ease than Brand. As Brand kept climbing his energy kept weakening, making him a bit out of breath by the time he finished.

Then they started to descend in the great beast. After a few turns and more descending, they reached the main command center. What a sight to see, a mixture of new and old combined together with elegant décor. It was fully automated to run off monitors with joysticks and mouses. While also being able to be control manually with the standard switches and knobs like traditional submarines. Truly a testimony of what mankind can achieve.

After being introduced to the Captain and his first mates, they were assigned rooms and would be contacted when meals would be served. It was a stark contrast to the much more friendly atmosphere on Captain Saul's ship. Most of the time was spent in their rooms, which for the size of the vessel, were quite small. On the other hand, the fact that they received private rooms is a statement by itself. On submarines, people have to be used to close quarters. Rarely does one get privacy, especially when sleeping.

Time travels differently when you don't see the sun or the moon. Just inside with no outside to orientate your local biological clock. It seemed to slow down as Brand spent most of his time with Bubba playing cards. To say how long that part of the trip had taken was hard, just that it felt much longer than it was.

The reasons they were on the submarine became evident when they finally arrived at the destination. As big as the submarine was, it became small when they surfaced in the cavern that was beyond huge. It was a Nazi base, but over the decades, it had turned into an American-German base, with the Nazis eventually going to the Moon. There were more than Americans and Germans there, but it was their base.

The advantages of having a base in Antarctica that can only be reached by submarines are obvious. Their arrival to Antarctica was unseen by the few who reside on the continent. Also, it has great defensive properties and is not affected by the weather. All the research done is private to the rest of the world.

It was there that they would meet the rest of their team and begin their journey to what was referred to as The Great One.

Chapter 24

THE GREAT ONE

The cavern was extensive, having almost everything you would expect in a small city. They were taken to a hotel and given rooms. Tomorrow they would meet the team and prepare to enter The Great One.

Once settled into their rooms, Bubba came knocking on Brand's door.

Bubba said to Brand, "This whole trip has been unreal, and I can't tell anyone?"

Brand giving a chuckle, responded, "First, you can't prove you even got here. Second even if you take pictures, everyone will think they are photoshopped. Third even with your story and pictures, who would believe you? And finally, that is if we live to tell about it!"

It was then that the realization of what was coming tomorrow hit Bubba.

"You can still change your mind. We can still go home, right?"

Brand, looking kindly at his friend, "No, I can not change my mind, but you still can!"

Now it was Bubba having a hard look on his face as he said, "No, we are in this together."

Brand responded, "Well, dinner is at nineteen hundred hours, and then get good sleep as tomorrow is going to be a big day."

The rest of the night was uneventful. They ate by themselves, of course, with Major Lee close by, and then went to their rooms for sleep.

Once Brand was done dinner and sitting in his room, trying to play out how he wanted tomorrow to go. He was used to working alone, and having a team with him made things that much more unpredictable.

One of his top concerns was keeping Bubba out of harm's way. Then hoping his hunch would work and he would be able to turn the force field off. If he was wrong, it would be his last mistake. Even if that happened, it would be an honorable exit, and in his mind, that mattered the most.

They met in a meeting room at six hundred hours, and introductions were made. There were three other members besides Brand, Bubba, and Major Lee. Brand mostly remembered people by their first name, for in small groups, that is all that is needed.

Also, Brand always studied the art of naming things. For example, America has a Defense Department but no Offense Department. It sounds bad to fund an Offense Department, but money is no issue if it is for Defense. The reality is that 95% of the Defense Department is Offense. Words have power and are used to affect the subconscious mind of the recipient.

Chance was his name. He was thin with a crew-cut hairstyle. He seemed bored and totally cold to everyone in the group. His official title was EOD, explosive ordnance disposal, meaning he was going to blow things up if he got the go-ahead and opportunity.

Of course, there was Major Lee, a survival expert, plus many other things. He was in his mid-thirties with total dedication to his operational orders. He seemed to care about the others, yet when needed, his primary orders would always supersede those around him.

Wescam was a communication and electronics expert. It would make sense he would be part of the group. If we were able to gain access he would be a great asset to the team. He was average height and weight with a well-trimmed mustache and beard. A very friendly person who cared about the team's success.

Bubba was there with no official title or duties to be done if they entered the target. Brand could see that Bubba was having the time of his life, that he had never experienced this part of what life has to offer. Regardless of what happens, as long as Bubba gets out of this alive, it will be one of the highlights of his life. Brand felt great in making that happen.

Brand's title was adviser, and was introduced as the key to getting them all inside. It was his job to unlock the door to The Great One. Once that was done, he would become like Bubba to the group. Having very little value except if they needed to get out.

Last but definitely not least was Roxanne, she had many degrees being an expert in pyramids, Antarctic and ancient cultures to name a few. Maybe it was her red hair which was beautiful, or her quiet commanding approach, she was a presence. She was average in height and slim, with a face that never needed makeup. A natural beauty that would make you forget how smart she was. She was a great asset to the team and being around her felt good.

They went over the details of how to get to The Great One and what functions would be performed by each member. By this point, everyone was eager to get there to begin except Brand. He didn't say anything but the way he envisioned it, in his mind, he would be the only one taking the initial risk.

The reality was if his hunch was wrong, it would mean his death.

Being in Antarctica and not even seeing the snow on top seemed odd, like seeing huge highways under the ice. Highways with four lanes, the tunnels were already there, and the roads were done by man. Also, in the tunnels, it felt warm for being in Antarctica, never going below 20 degrees Fahrenheit. They drove there in a large RV which was also their base camp when they arrived. The drive was over two hours, and not much was said during the trip.

Brand seemed to be relaxed for someone going to his potential death. He had peace in what he was going to try to do. That was important to him concerning his death. He wanted to be in control of it. Not some slow-moving disease that creeps up and defeats you without a noble purpose to die for. This would work either way.

After what he did for Hector, he now felt bad. If he had only killed Gaylord, that would have been ok, but so many others died, also. How long before judgment with how many more deaths to be guilty of?

Worst case, it would be fast. The flash drive was very clear, maybe two to three seconds until it was complete. Death would probably be shorter than that, with the last one or two seconds being the aftermath.

When they arrived, Brand was surprised there were no guards. Then again, with so few people on the continent and the only way to get there via the road they were on, it was secure. They had seen no other vehicles on their way there, and the tunnels were monitored by cameras, as was the site.

The Great One lived up to its name. It was huge with a shimmering metallic color that was reflected by the energy field surrounding it. There was a ramp leading up to a doorway that was shaped like a triangle. It was a huge door with the top point being 20 feet high and the doorway being 6 feet wide at the center.

As they were walking up the ramp which led to the door, Brand suggested firmly that they all stayed back until he opened the door. No one disagreed, and they waited about 4 feet behind Brand. As he stood in front of the door, he heard footsteps behind him.

Bubba was a few inches from his back as he said, "Got your back."

Then Major Lee came to the left of Brand, a few more inches away than Bubba. It seemed time had stopped for not more than a second later Wescam and Roxanne were up next to the left of Bubba. Chance did not move. Everyone was a few inches apart except for Chance.

Brand seemed to be in a trance with his eyes closed, and now the time seemed like forever. All except Chance were excited to hopefully get in. There was a group feeling without reason that they would succeed where the others had failed.

Brand then said, "Hate to say this, but we are going to have to wait a bit."

Now Chance became alive and, with a smiling grin, said, "It's alright, just say it you're scared!"

Bubba with a roar, "Kid, that's the bravest man you will ever meet!"

Brand seemed unaffected by Chance's statement and replied calmly, "I am not scared. Only people afraid of dying would be. It's just not time yet."

Major Lee jumped in, "When will it be time?"

Brand replied with a shrug of his shoulders, "Don't know, maybe minutes or hours. I suggest we go back to the RV, and when I am ready, we will get in."

Chapter 25

SECOND TRY

Sam Smith and Nina Woodhall were watching and hearing all that transpired, with Nina asking Sam, "What do you think? Why did he stop?"

Sam responded with one word, "Disappointing."

Colonel Bolt was also watching in his office, having totally different thoughts about what just happened. Thinking to himself that Bubba was right on target, Brand had gone into the most dangerous situations, never running away from the action. Bolt was not impatient, figuring that Brand had something up his sleeve and would strike when the time is right.

Usually, when Brand contacts Chameleon, there were no delays or issues, and they seemed to step outside of Earth's time and discuss different aspects or feelings regarding life. Sometimes Brand would be getting educated by Chameleon, for its knowledge was greater than vast.

This time when he was at The Great One's door trying to contact Chameleon, there was a problem. They communicated telepathically, with Chameleon telling Brand he was busy. Brand countering that he really needed his help in his time. When dealing with an eternal life form, time is totally different than normal people who have death always waiting.

Chameleon said it would be as quick as possible to get back to Brand. Dealing with powers that are great, negotiations don't usually work, so the conversation was over. That is when Brand told the group it would happen, just later.

When they were back in the RV, the minutes became long hours. The long hours became many as hope for the success of the mission died.

Roxanne came over to Brand, saying, "I believe in you, and when you're ready, we will get in."

Brand knew she was trying to console him, and he was touched. He had let the group down, with just Roxanne and Bubba being sympathetic about it.

The only one happy was Chance. His grin was the opposite of the group's feelings, except for Brand, who seemed relaxed and enjoying the extra time given. As they passed the 8-hour mark of waiting, Brand suggested they get some sleep, and hopefully, tomorrow would be the day. Gloom filled the spirits of everyone else except Bubba, Chance, and Roxy.

In the 17th hour, Brand announced he was ready.

Brand, with eager excitement, said, "All right, let's go. Let's find out what is in that pyramid." Everyone was taken by surprise yet ready to find out if Brand could get them in.

They approached the doorway again with everyone in the same spots as before. This time Bubba put his hand on Brand's right shoulder, saying, "Got your back!"

Then Major Lee put his hand on Brand's left shoulder and, without saying anything, gave Brand a look that said we are in this together. Roxanne wrapped her right arm around Bubba left arm, with Wescam holding Roxanne's hand. This time everyone was touching except Chance.

Now they would find out the answer together. In such a short time, they had bonded as a team. Brand understood this, as he would have done the same in their spots. Either you trust your teammates, or you don't. That trust is shown in actions, never words. That is why when your commander gives you orders, you do it without question. It can be summed up in just one word, trust.

As touched as Brand was with that action of his companions, he said, "I very much appreciate your actions, but I think it is wiser if I do this alone." With that, Major Lee and Bubba removed their hands from Brand as he prepared to push the button.

Brand stretched his arm, so his hand was near the small triangle where the button resided within. As he put his hand near the button, Chameleon turned into a translucent silver hand that extended from Brand's hand and then tried to get through the energy field.

Brand thought it would be easy for Chameleon to do. Also, he did not expect to feel in any way what Chameleon was feeling. Both thoughts were wrong. Chameleon was struggling to overtake the energy field, it was like a tug of war or arm wrestling. Brand could feel Chameleon winning, then losing and winning again. Somewhere in Brand's thoughts, he knew Chameleon would need to win soon or his energy would be depleted to nothing.

Time to Brand had stopped as he had no reference to how long this struggle lasted. It seemed like a very long time. Then what was one last major effort of energy, Chameleon's hand touched the button, and the field went down. It was no victory as Chameleon was almost out of energy and there would be no telling how long, if ever, it would regain its powers. Even the tattoo on Brand's arm disappeared. For all practical purposes, Chameleon had died to get them in.

Brand had no time to mourn as he instinctively knew the field would not be down for long. He shouted to the group to move now as he went through the doorway.

To everyone watching Brand and his translucent silver hand, they were glowing from a low intensity to a higher intensity while also changing colors. It was easy to see it on the hand, but Brand also had a light-changing glow. It lasted for almost 10 minutes before Brand shouted the order to "Let's go!"

All went through the doorway, with Chance being the last to enter. After 30 seconds, the energy field went back on.

Sam and Nina were watching a recording of the event.

Sam looked at Nina and asked, "What do you think?"

Nina replied, "That man has more lives than a cat."

Sam nodded in approval, "Exactly."

Bolt also saw the event in real-time as he kept monitoring during the 17-hour delay, waiting. Bolt's thoughts as they entered the pyramid were pleased that Subject 9 made it through.

Chapter 26

THE 4th DIMENSION

Once the group had entered the doorway, it felt like they were traveling through a short passageway. After about 3 feet, the doorway disappeared, and they were outside. Now there was total confusion within the group about what just happened.

When they looked up, there were clouds with a blueish-violet sky. They were in a semi-rain forest with many shades of green all around them. There was a stone walkway that had a purple glow about it. The trees and plants looked as they do on Earth, with the greens being an intense shade in color. Major Lee was first to ask, and as he did, he looked straight at Brand.

"What just happened? Where did the pyramid go? Where are we?"

All eyes were on Brand as he spoke, "First, you're welcome for making it into the pyramid. I think I know what happened, but it is only speculation." He looked at the faces that were looking at him. Brand continued, "This is only a guess, and it will take your heads some time to wrap around it. Does anyone know about the 4th dimension?"

Major Lee answered, "The dimension of time?"

Brand continuing, "That is the popular belief, but it is wrong. Time exists in every dimension. It is an attribute of dimensions.

The 4th dimension is space inside and outside of the third dimension." Now seeing that no one understood what he was referring to he try to explain with more detail.

Brand started again, "Imagine a box and then a bigger box outside of that box. Then imagine a smaller box inside the box in the center. So you have three boxes each within the next. Now imagine that you can't see it, but they are all connected. We live in the 3rd dimension and can only see the box in the center without seeing the outside or inside boxes. Does that make it clearer?"

No one spoke, but then Wescam said, "So we are now in the outside box?"

Brand was beaming, "Exactly!" As if that cleared up the entire situation.

Wescam then asked, "So now what?" Which was the question on everyone's mind.

Brand responded, "I imagine that the pyramid is somewhere out here. We just have to search for it."

Chance now spoke and was visibly scared. His voice cracked, "How do we get back to our dimension? What happened to the door we came through?"

Brand now looking into Chance's eyes, asked, "Why do you ask? Are you scared? We still need to get into the pyramid in this dimension. As for getting home, I am thinking it will be in the pyramid when we find the inside space." Brand kept his eyes directly locked on Chance, just waiting.

Chance just stood there with his mouth slightly opened. His eyes were dazed, slowly understanding the reality of their situation.

Brand now not caring about being polite, ask again with a smirk, "If you're scared, you can stay close to me!"

Major Lee then redirected the conversation to what was important, asking, "Where do you think it is located?" Which was directed at Brand.

"I imagine it will be very big, probably bigger than what we saw in Antarctica. Someone needs to climb a tree, and hopefully, we will see it or at least see how to get out of this forest."

Major Lee agreed that was logical except for climbing the tree. They had two drones, using the first to hopefully locate the pyramid. Obviously, everyone's backpacks were not supplied with the same resources. Brand and Bubba's backpacks did not have a drone.

Wescam tried the communication equipment, but it did not work, at least not where they currently were located. Roxanne had been quiet, yet she did not look nervous. She had the eyes of an explorer who was not worried about the return trip. Just enjoying all the newness around her.

Bubba looked amazed, like someone who now knows a truth that others never would know or believe. This is what Bubba had always wanted to do, and now he was here doing it. He kept Brand always close in sight, not for protection but to protect his friend that had made his dreams come true. He knew money could get you a lot of things, but it could not buy you this type of adventure.

Roxanne's thoughts were on the five men around her. Poor Chance was obviously scared, and Brand had pleasure in pounding on it. Bubba was the nicest and most out-of-place person there. She had a fondness for him compared to the others. Wescam who was nice but all business. Then there was Major Lee and Brand. Her intuition told her they were both killers, dangerous men that were different than the rest of the team.

In Brand's case, he seemed relaxed the entire time. When they had trouble getting through the door the first and second time and now here, wherever that was, he seemed like he was on vacation. There were so many questions that surrounded that man. How did he get them past the doorway? That question was not even brought up because of the situation after it. And he was 20 years her senior without seeming it, not just because his hair was brown. It was his eyes, they were bright and compelling, and his energy seemed stronger than a man of his age should have. Also, it was assumed that if they made entry into the pyramid, Major Lee would be in command. Yet Brand seemed more in control of the group than before they had entered the structure.

Last, Major Lee showed no fear but was tensed in body and careful in his words.

She stayed closed to Bubba, who she trusted and like the best. She was not overly concerned about her current predicament, which seemed strange to herself. There was so much to learn that her natural curiosity overtook her fears.

The drone worked, and they were on the fringe of the forest with a grassland past that. There in the distance was a pyramid looking to be about 5 miles away, but it was hard to tell given the size of the structure. The plan was to get as close as possible and then camp for the night and try to enter the pyramid in the morning after sleep. This was decided by Major Lee and Brand with no objections from the rest.

They made their way out of the forest to the grasslands with little problems. Everything was like Earth, but inside the pyramid, they had first entered. It was a world within a structure. As they proceeded through the grasslands, everyone was adjusting to the new reality they were in.

Brand was used to walking Sweetbull about 7 miles a day. His watch registered close to 50 miles a week. The path was easy to travel. They had many breaks, for as they got closer, the pyramid was so large that it seemed just a couple of hours away. They wanted to rest before the next stage, so there was no rush.

Brand had two packs of smokes with him and was smoking at least once per hour. Major Lee was at point with Wescam and Roxanne behind him. Then Chance, Brand, and Bubba finishing the line.

There were animals and flowers, all things you would see and smell on Earth, just no people. It truly was beautiful, nature left to its own. The air had a crispness, and it felt like there was more oxygen in each breath compared to Earth.

The hike was no problem for all members as they moved closer to their objective. During one of their stop breaks, they formed into three groups, and their conversation were simultaneously spoken. One group was Brand and Chance, another Roxanne and Bubba, with the third being Major Lee and Wescam.

Chance started the conversation, "I was wrong. You don't seem scared of anything."

Brand replied with a smile, "Have a secret weapon, old age, and don't want to die in bed."

Chance smiled, "Do you know how to get back to the 3rd dimension?"

The answer was short, "Of course."

Roxanne asked Bubba, "How did Brand get us into the pyramid?"

Bubba looked like who knows and replied, "I have seen a lot of things I can't explain when in his company. This will be added to them." And with that had a big smile.

Roxanne then, looking concerned, asked, "So you think we will get out of this alive?"

Bubba put his huge arm around her shoulders and leaned in closer while almost whispering and said, "I promise you, Brand will get us home!"

Wescam standing with Major Lee, asked the Major, "Do you think we will get out of here?"

Major Lee, without moving, said, "I didn't think we would get into here."

As they got relatively close and had set up camp, Brand wanted to address the group.

Brand began, "I want to tell you a story. When I was training for SCUBA, there was a procedure called Ditch and Dive. All your gear is thrown to the bottom of the pool, and all you have to do is dive down and put it all on before you rise to the surface. Of course, getting your regulator is the first step. Well, I could not see, the chlorine blinded me, and I had trouble finding the regulator. I was out of breath when my hand finally found it. Without air, I had to rise to the surface and fail the test. I was 3 feet before the surface when I realized the regulator was in my mouth, and all I had to do was breathe. Fear will bring panic, and panic will kill you or someone around you. We are going to deal with things we know nothing about. Their science will seem like magic, and all that unknown is like darkness. You all have to eliminate the fear that your imagination will bring to your minds. Once that is done, then you will be able to handle it."

Now he looked at the group before him and continued, "I believe in each of you, not just that but trust you with my life. We will survive this and look back with a smile. Get sleep, knowing that one of us is always on watch. Tomorrow we deal with the unknown without fear."

They were all speechless, just looking at him. It reminded him of when he gave a presentation about space in college, and when it came time for questions, there were none. Was his presentation that good or bad? Who knows?

Bubba came up to Brand, saying, "You never stop!"
Brand, looking puzzled, "What."
Bubba responded, "Amazing me, my friend."

Chapter 27

DECISIONS MADE

As they approached the pyramid, it was incredible. Not built of rock, it had an amazing metallic surface that shimmered with different colors as if a breeze was blowing on it. Brand imagined that it could show images and could handle four different groups of viewers, one on each side. The lights changed as they approached into geometric patterns, with light moving in and out of itself within the patterns.

The effect was mesmerizing, like the building was acknowledging their presence. They had not seen any people. There was a river to the left of them, about 3 miles away. A ramp led to the doorway, which was not hidden. This time there seemed to be no energy field, yet Brand still wanted a minute to get ready.

As they arrived at the door, Brand went to touch it, but before his hand could get near the door, it just disappeared. Higher technology is always amazing, even when your own technology is impressive.

Maybe it was just a hologram you could tell yourself if you tried to explain it. The truth is it looked very solid but disappeared completely when they were close to it. And that is also a trait of higher science. Even simple things like a door are different than you would expect or need to be.

In a way, it was a wake-up call to the group that they should expect the unexpected. Now at the doorway, there was a disagreement between Major Lee and Brand. One wanted some of the party to wait at the door, while the other wanted all to enter and stay together.

Roxanne, hearing her name being used, decided she would become a part of the discussion. She began with, "Gentlemen, I think I have a say on where I go!"

Brand turning her way, "You are exactly correct. In this case, I propose that we all enter and stay together while in the pyramid."

Major Lee then asserted, "It would be more prudent and safer to split our forces while one group guards this door and the others do a quick recon."

Roxanne looked at the two men who wanted to decide her future. There was a bit of anger in that look. She always had to prove she was better and tougher than her male counterparts. Now all were looking and waiting for her response.

"All of us have put our lives on the line for this moment. The decision should be a personal one. We each have earned it!"

In theory, Major Lee should have had complete control once they entered the pyramid. That is the theory, yet Brand's influence on the group never ended at the door. The unspoken thoughts of all were they needed Brand to get out of the 4th dimension.

Major Lee conceded to Roxanne, and each member was given a choice to stay until the reconnaissance was over or to go into the pyramid. Brand was used to studying people, so this incident was no different. He could tell that Major Lee was a man who picked his fights. Someone who is tough enough that he does not have to win each encounter, focusing strictly on the final objective.

When the tally was done, all would go in together. Even Chance, who now stayed close to Brand all the time. It is funny how things can change so quickly in group dynamics. For whatever reasons, they were now truly acting as a team.

Brand was trying to keep a positive feeling even though his instincts were screaming danger. Yet now he was part leader of this group, and how he behaved mattered. Getting in was easy in his mind, which didn't work out well. Going into the 4th dimension was not part of the plan. How exactly to get out? He really did not have any clear thoughts on that. Staying confident was key to everyone's mental well-being. Hopefully, a way out would be revealed.

Bolt had contacted Nina to set up a call with Sam Smith. Once the video call was established, there were Nina and Sam in Sam's office with Bolt in his own.

Bolt started with, "I think we should set up a company at the door, so if the field goes down, they can go in to help."

Sam looking a bit pale, replied, "The strange thing is I was thinking the same thing! I'll have two companies ready if the opportunity happens."

Bolt seemed very pleased with that news like he was expecting an argument that never happened.

Nina was watching both men in shock. Don't they realize that if they both had the same feeling, maybe it wasn't really their feeling? It seemed to her they were both being manipulated.

The call ended, and Sam told her to make it happen. Four hundred of the best fighting men and women would be ready if the energy field went down.

As they entered the structure, the first thing that became apparent, it was designed for beings much bigger than their size. The ceilings were 25 to 30 feet tall. Doorways were least 15 feet high. The walls were similar to the outside, providing a glow of light that seemed to move with them during their wandering. It would change colors subtly yet was pleasing to all.

The structure was huge, with their passage just being the main hallway to many other chambers on each side. There were many strange ramps that traveled at 45-degree angles intercepting other hallways and rooms. It became obvious that if not careful, it would be easy to get lost in this great machine.

Certain doors did not disappear, which made them assume they were locked. Other rooms had what you would expect, one being a banquet room, just that all the items were much larger than what a standard person would need. The chairs were huge, and the table top was 7 feet from the floor.

They started to relax as there were many great and strange sights but no living beings. Not even any animals or plants, for that matter. It seemed empty, but that was just an illusion. They had been taking pictures and audio notes plus trying to leave markings to find their way out.

In Brand's mind, the markings were just to make them feel good. The only way to get out is to find the door that leads there, not backtracking to where they had been. What Brand was searching for was the command center. He figured there must be a central area where most of the controls are located. Find that area, then disable the energy field while also hoping to find the door back to Antarctica.

It is funny how the mind thinks, how some far-away thoughts will just jump into one's current attention. Just as he was thinking how impossible his plan was, he remembered a college professor he had for quantitative business analysis. They always called it QBA, yet it really was just a class on statistics.

They would deal with huge probabilities that would almost never happen. Like winning a huge lottery three times in a row each time it was drawn. The odds of that are so large against it that you might think it could never happen. It would be stated that 1 out of, some huge number, is the probability of that event happening.

Yet this professor said something that Brand would never forget, *one does happen!* Yes, his plan's success was a crazy long shot, but one does happen. In this case, the lives of his companions were betted on it.

Brand's thoughts went to the Great Pyramid in Egypt and to the model he made as a young man. The Queen's chamber is centered and at the right height being 2/3 below the top. That was the spot he was searching for in The Great One.

It would seem fairly easy to get there, but it was not. First, he did not realize how big the structure was and exactly what level they were at. With all those limitations, that was the goal of Brand's quest. Whether through luck or a good sense of direction, he finally found the control room.

The room had a different look than most of the others they had seen. There was a long console angled with three chairs facing it. It was sunken to the rest of the surroundings forming a half circle. The floor panels were different in that area and completed the other half of the circle.

Now that Brand had found the area he was searching for, it felt anti-climactic. There still were no people, and the room had no switches or anything that would activate it.

It was decided that they would eat and camp there for the night. No one yet had asked Brand what was on everyone's mind. How do we get out of the 4th dimension and return to Antarctica. Brand thought that exact question. When it came to getting in, everything was based on Chameleon. Now with Chameleon dead or close to it, getting out was anything but obvious.

Brand always found problems that seemed unanswerable were much easy to handle after sleep. They set 4-hour watches with two people doing the watch while the others sleep.

Brand pulled Bubba to the side for a private exchange. Brand was serious in mood, which was the opposite compared to most of the journey.

Brand looking intently into Bubba's eyes, "I am giving you a mission which is extremely important. Do you accept?"

Bubba was a guest for the whole trip compared to everyone else. Each person had a purpose when their time would come. He was eager to accept but did not know the protocols for such things.

With a smile on his face asked, "Do I have to accept before I know what it is?"

Brand, still very serious, responded, "No, I will tell you, and then you can accept or decline. But if you accept there will be things you may not want to do, you will still need to do them!" As he was speaking to Bubba, it reminded Brand of how he describes being a man. Doing all the things you don't want to do. That is why it's always a hard job.

Bubba waited patiently, his eyes not leaving Brand's view.

Brand continued, "When I figure out how to get back to the 3rd dimension, I need you to make sure that you, Chance, Wescam, and Roxanne leave. Chance will go gladly, and not sure about Wescam. Roxanne will not want to leave. I don't care if you have to carry her over your back. Even if she is screaming she wants to stay, you make sure you all leave! Understood?"

Brand then said, "It is extremely vital the outside knows what is going on in here!"

Bubba looking solemn, replied, "I got it. What about you and Major Lee?"

Brand answered, "We have a different mission."

Observing becomes a habit that leads to quantifying and then judging. Brand had spent decades watching people as they respond to different circumstances. In its most simplistic expression is the run or fight syndrome. Yet there are so many more subtle actions people will do that once you have trained your eyes to observe and then recall past observations, you can almost predict their future actions. Everyone is different, and it is not a science, yet after time, study, and practice, Brand felt comfortable with his assessments.

As Brand watched Roxanne and Bubba, he could tell they were fond of each other's company. They had stayed closed from the beginning of the expedition. Now they always were together. He could tell she felt safe with Bubba.

In that regard, when you know you're around killers, there is a different vibration in the air. Especially if you have never killed someone, they have done the ultimate action that says this can never be undone. Most people will never kill someone because that feeling that this can't be fixed is enough to stop them. Not for killers.

There was no doubt that Major Lee had killed, and Brand chuckled to himself because he also fit that group. Chance had killed, but as a coward does, with bombs. Then there were Bubba and Roxanne, who had never killed anything. It seemed obvious by their actions and words.

Wescam confused Brand as he was hard to peg on just about anything. He reminded Brand about his youth as being likable by all and mysterious. The reality was Brand was not likable, yet there were many similarities between the two.

After most had sleep they were at a loss on exactly what to focus on, that was when the great computer made its appearance.

Chapter 28

ADAM

It represented the people who had created it, they were called the First People. Explaining that the form they were viewing was a hologram with mass. It had started the awakening process for those that were left after the disaster.

The hologram alien was 12 feet tall with the same general body parts as a human. It was more muscular than the average person. Looking like a bodybuilder with six fingers and toes. It also had a larger jaw, and its head looked bigger than a person's should be. Having two rows of teeth and was dressed in what reminded him of Greek and Egypt styles.

It spoke in English and wanted to exchange questions with the group. They referred to the entity as Adam.

Before that began, it was suggested that they take a patch that would help them to speak the First People's language and understand things around them better. It would be placed behind the ear and works its way into the head. There it resides in your brain and could be described like having a chip with information feeding your brain and doing other calculations and translations.

Brand, Major Lee and Wescam wanted the patch, while Bubba, Roxanne, and Chance absolutely did not. The patch itself was large, being about a 1 and ½ inch radius. Once it was attached above the top of the ear, it started to work its way in. Hair and skull did not seem to impede its progress. After about 5 minutes and a slight bit of pain, like a migraine headache, it was operational.

Adam started with, "How did you get past the energy field?"

Brand always liked to take control in situations like this and instantly answered with, "It was easy."

Adam continued, "How did you do it?"

Brand answered, still with cockiness, "Just matched the frequency vibrational energy needed to pass through it and pushed the button."

Now it appeared Adam was evaluating this answer, as it probably was correct but still did not address the real issue. They were playing a game of logic where all answers have to be true, but they don't have to help answer the question.

Brand now asked his question, "Some of my friends want to leave. Will you help them to leave now?"

This question took many in the group by surprise, except Major Lee.

Adam was a proper host and countered, "Of course, if they want to leave, they can. This is not a prison. Once the First People are revived, I know they would like to meet you all. After that happens, I promise to help them leave."

After some more questions back and forth from all members except Bubba and Chance, Adam conveyed that he would like to tell the story of the First People.

Adam began, "Back at the beginning of time when the universe was young, we began to understand the nature of all around us. Science and philosophy combined with spiritual thoughts and humility we created structure and helped life coexist with each other. We traveled to many stars helping planets develop. Their societies bearing great influence from our culture.

When we landed on this planet, there was little structure to be seen. We started developing many great structures reflecting the planet and the universe while providing function. You would call it this planet's golden age. We were in harmony with the local inhabitants, plus created a very pleasant environment for ourselves, while keeping harmony and balance with the planet.

Most of our people were outside this ship when the great shift happened. It was incredibly fast, and within minutes everything was frozen. The people within this structure were put into zero-time sleep units until the problems could be resolved.

I have been monitoring this world and its progress toward perfect balance. The Atlanteans were just a tiny reflection of what we had accomplished. And as time continued, it became worst. The Egyptians were but a shadow of the Atlanteans having a fraction of what we had started with. Now your present empires have some secrets but also all the properties of culture too young in mind to understand harmony's balance, while also missing some of the most important science and culture needed for that balance."

That speech had left everyone speechless, even Brand, which does not happen often. Finally, after what seemed to be very long, Major Lee thanked Adam for the information. Then almost everyone did the same thing at the same moment, all with an earnestness that made it even more funny hearing all their voices at once saying "Thank you."

Adam was really a perfect host, and if the First People were like him, then everything should be fine. That was what most of the group was thinking.

Roxanne asked Adam, "Mr. Adam, how long before we will meet the inhabitants of this ship?"

Adam happily replied, "Very soon, I have awakened just 50. Two members at a time. With 20-minute intervals. They should be arriving in about 4 minutes.

Brand had a suspicion about Adam, which he was keeping to himself. This would turn out to make a huge difference in what was to follow. Human nature really goes beyond the word Human. For what is observed in Humans can be seen in many other forms. Things are usually not what they seem.

Chapter 29

THIATIS

When the first person from the First People arrived, he was the complete opposite of Adam. He came angrily into the command center with his full attention on Adam.

Only Major Lee, Brand, and Wescam could understand the conversation, while the others without the patch could not. The patch did more than translation as now all the controls were being explained within their heads. Now all three men knew how to stop the energy field and open the door back to the Antarctic.

Thiatis stormed into the room, "Why have we been in the chamber for thousands of years!?"

Adam, with a calmness, "The world is not ready yet, and more than that, you are not ready."

That only made Thiatis angrier, "How dare you judge me. We created you!"

Adam answered, "You had nothing to do with my creation. The people who created me had beauty and light. You were in the structure for learning and have not yet learned to be what your potential is."

Thiatis, now enraged, yelled, "Deactivate yourself right now!"

Adam looked him in the eyes with, "No."

Now the man and android were both working the controls as some needed physical interaction. Brand and the group had moved to the corner near the door they had entered to get to the control room. Major Lee and Brand were in front with Wescam, then Bubba and Roxanne with Chance in the back.

They were angled about 45 degrees to view the action between Thiatis and Adam. That is when Thiatis pulled out his weapon, which looked like a sword, but it was huge. Six feet long and 5 inches wide. It had a moving type of metal, which made the blade look like it was in constant motion.

He swung the sword, which ripped through Adam, causing damage. He must have known that when swinging it yet still doing it out of rage.

Then he shouted at Adam, "What are these rodents doing in the ship, in the control room, and they have patches!"

Adam tried to respond, but it was obvious he was having difficulty with his functions after the sword attack. Finally, saying as if the question was foolish, "They are guests, a lower form but not rodents. As a guest, they were offered patches." The speech was broken, and the sound varied in many tones.

It was then that Thiatis put his full attention on the visitors or intruders, depending on your perspective.

At that moment, Major Lee, Brand, and Wescam had a mini-huddle.

Wescam said, "If I can get to the right side of the console, I think I can deactivate the energy field. The teleport to Antarctica is not far from that. We all know this and where the pad is. But I will need time to get it right!"

Brand responded, "Sounds good. Once done, get them to the pad and go yourself. The Major and I will stay."

Major Lee shook his head up and down in full agreement.

Brand then said, "When he comes over here, the Major and I are going to cause a distraction. Wescam, that's your window."

They had set up a command center relatively close to the Great One with some protection but not much. The teams were ready and just waiting for the field to go down. They had power vehicles and all sorts of equipment as long as it would fit through the opening.

Even though there was no communication that the field would be going down, there was a feeling among the crew and command, that it would happen. Everyone was on a ready state, as soon as it was disabled, they were heading in for action.

Thiatis was coming over with bad intentions, which was obvious. With Adam, even though his size was huge, he did not feel menacing. Thiatis was very different. He was near them within seconds, his wide stride closing the gap quickly. In his right hand was his 6-foot sword, now in an arch, swinging down to kill Major Lee and probably others with one blow.

Major Lee shot off a mini burst of fire, as his weapon was in hand. The bullets seemed to disappear in a personal force field that Thiatis wore. Then seconds later, Brand also was firing at Thiatis too. With both their bullets hitting his force field almost simultaneously, it pushed him back away from them.

Then Brand and Major Lee separated forming a triangle with Thiatis at the top. Their plan to distract him was working yet it felt this would only work for a short time before more First People would arrive.

Adam seemed concerned like he had made a misjudgment. To him, the lesser forms of life were never a threat. He would have to take corrective actions immediately.

Now Adam and Thiatis were on the same page. They were awakening all the First People that were left on the ship.

Brand and Major Lee had now moved to a spot that for Thiatis to see them would allow a blind spot for Wescam to make his move. Brand wanted his full attention, so he started his distraction.

Brand began with, "Things can be different than they seem. Must say I don't like being called a rodent. I think you owe me an apology." This was all said in Thiatis language without having to think about it. The patch was truly amazing.

It reminded Brand about civilization, that technology outpaces the intellect of those who wield it. Their science was truly very high, but their emotional control was not close. Of course, Brand was baiting Thiatis trying to keep his focus on Brand.

Adam was having more difficulties and now was barely able to keep form. More First People were going to show up shortly.

Major Lee was now guarding Bubba, Roxanne, and Chance. The mood had changed drastically, and most were now fearful for their lives. As Wescam worked on the controls and Brand kept moving slightly closer to Thiatis, which seemed to distress him. Maybe his personal energy field was weakening. It felt like forever, yet Wescam actually disabled the field and started the teleport pad within a minute.

Major Lee gave Brand the signal that Wescam was finished. Now Brand and Major Lee wanted to keep Thiatis from the door where their friends would escape.

Wescam moved fast, and in seconds he was with the group by the door. Then, Chance, Roxanne, and Bubba followed Wescam out of the control room. Wescam was leading them around a curving hallway to what looked like a platform extending out from the hallway.

There were no lights or anything that would make it look special. Wescam told them to enter the platform, and it will take them to the ramp at the Great One. Chance, without hearing another word, ran to the platform and was gone instantly.

Now Roxanne started to talk, "What about Major Lee and-" Bubba picked her up and started walking to the platform.

Roxanne, who was quite upset with that, shouted, "What are you doing?"

Bubba responded, "Following orders."

Roxanne tried to get out of his grip as her feet were off the floor, "Who's orders?"

Bubba's answer was, "Brand's orders."

Roxanne, with disbelief in her voice plus anger, "He can't give-"

At that point, Bubba had entered the platform, and they were both gone.

Wescam could hear more First People entering the control room and Major Lee firing what sounded like a full clip. Usually, that happens when a man gets scared. You just keep your finger pulled tight on that trigger for as long as the bullets will fly.

Wescam thought, the platform to life or the control room to death. He hesitated for a few seconds and then ran.

Thiatis had activated all the sleeping chambers to awaken instantly. Currently, there were four of the First People against two low life form invaders. They will make quick work of them, with the entire planet being next.

Chapter 30

THE BATTLE

It was looking bad for Major Lee and Brand. The Major had emptied his clip and was reloading while Brand was now firing his full clip. As the First People were just within reach of the Major and Brand, Wescam came running back and opened fire, also shooting a full clip. The First People were not killed but were pushed back upon each other.

Major Lee had reloaded, but more First People were entering the room, and the outcome was already known. Not if they could survive but how long before they were all killed.

Chance and then Bubba, holding Roxanne in a bear hug, popped into existence in front of the door at The Great One's ramp. They were a bit disoriented, and a few soldiers quickly moved them from the ramp to the command center.

The field was off, and soldiers were piling through the doorway of the pyramid with great speed and organized urgency. Four soldiers at a time every second, they just keep surging through the doorway.

Bubba had tears in his eyes as Bolt came up to him.

Bolt looked Bubba in the eyes and said, "We'll get him out."

Bubba responded, "He ordered me to leave and take Roxanne." Now Bubba was showing signs of shock as his speech had slowed down considerably. They moved him over to a table with chairs, had him sit, and wrapped him in a blanket.

Roxanne was now feeling bad giving Bubba a hard time as he was definitely traumatized by the whole affair. She went over to him, holding his hand gently. There are times when no words can equal the simple touch of another person.

Wescam and Major Lee and Brand were grouped together waiting for the final attack by The First People. Their swords could also fire power bolts, which seemed like a ball of electricity that exploded on contact.

Brand had the feeling that they were going to attach from all sides, just organizing how their attack would begin. There were over ten now in the room, creating a half circle around Brand's group. It felt like The First People were just playing with them now, enjoying their discomfort until they would issue the final blow.

The end would not be long. Just then, Wescam wandered too far from the Major and Brand and was shot with an electric bolt. His arm, from the elbow down, was now just a mingle of blood, flesh, and bone. He did not show any pain, but it was horrible to see. It would only be a few seconds now before their end when the most unexpected thing happened.

They had been guarding the doorway that led to the transport pad. The control room had many entryways, with the room now having over 50 First People in the area.

That is when the cavalry arrived. Seeing those brave soldiers rushing into the room with their weapons blazing was amazing. The first ones were hit with the energy bolts and went down, but others behind them kept racing in.

Soon they were spread out and had better firepower than what Brand's group had. After multiple direct shots in succession, the First People's force field would go down, and then they could be destroyed.

The soldiers were taking great losses but were holding the First People from advancing to the doorway they were protecting.

Now some soldiers were taking the wounded out to the transport. Wescam was taken by two soldiers who accompanied him to the transport to make sure he stepped on it.

Bolt, Bubba, and Roxanne were now on the landing in front of The Great One, where people were popping up from being in the pyramid. They were all wounded. Most severely was Wescam popping up with his left mangled arm that was blood, bone, and skin all destroyed from the elbow down.

Even with the terrible injuries, the soldiers kept going through the door. Bubba now realized how brave these people were and how committed they were to the country's safety. The three of them waited and watched for Brand and Major Lee to return.

As the battle kept raging, new defenses and offenses were used. It is during these periods that no one knows who is really going to win. Then usually, something different, or significant happens and tilts the balance to one side.

The floor was full of bodies, mostly dead but others dying. It was to the point that it became hard to walk, and both sides were stuck in their positions. Then the First People used a different weapon than before, which changed the stalemate.

The best way to describe it would be a goo that moved on its own and could not be killed with bullets. It would recombine and continue on toward the soldiers. When the goo touched the skin, it would burn and work like acid, making a hole as it moved.

Positions were now being rearranged, and what soldiers were left alive were falling back. Brand and Major Lee were pinned down for a couple of reasons. Both were injured, with Major Lee close to death. Brand's right leg was hit with an energy blast which seemed to have broken his leg, with possibly his hip and ankle also shattered.

The battle was again nearing a conclusion when the Major said to Brand, "It's been an honor."

Brand looking at his dying companion, "Major, it's been my honor."

For whatever reason, the goo had not come near them, which made Brand happy. Then the thought of being happy in a place like where he was, made him smile. Funny how the mind can juggle so many different aspects and come out with a conclusion that seems crazy.

Just as the end was approaching, another change happened that was completely unexpected. Four beams of light blueish-purple in color appeared around Brand and the Major. They formed a semi-circle spaced about 5 feet apart. Then the next moment, there were 20 beings in the room.

Brand had seen them before, yet these were the soldiers of their races. Ten Dragon Men and ten Large Greys all had weapons and what appeared to be body armor. The Dragon Men looked like large reptilian creatures being 10 feet tall and having scales that were gold and brown that could be seen. They wore suits that had metal and were jointed so they could move. Their weapons were laser in design, shooting short bursts of energy. The Greys were 7 to 8 feet tall and also wore a type of body armor that was more flexible than the Dragon Men. They had weapons more similar to the First People yet seemed more destructive to nonbiological life forms.

This assault was different than the humans' attack. They were taking shots at certain equipment in the room. The Greys were shooting the equipment while the Dragon Men attacked the First People.

Technology is a double edge sword. The more it can do, the easier it is to brake. There is always a soft spot that, once destroyed, can bring the rest of it down.

Chapter 31

TIME TO GO

There was a change in the environment. The walls, floors, and ceilings were pulsating. It was like it was breathing in and out. First, the floor would sink and then bubble up, repeating the process. As time proceeded, the fluctuations became more severe.

Then the exodus began. The human military started to retreat, sending soldiers to the teleport pad, which sent them back to the ramp at The Great One. The First People were leaving the room as there were many teleport pads located around the outside of the control room. The Dragon men and the Greys also left via the light which reappeared over them. It was the same blueish-purple light but working in reverse.

Brand was pinned down by many dead bodies of all different races, with his leg unable to move. The thought of yelling for help never entered his mind. The instability of the structure was now getting extremely violent, making it feel the end was near. This would be a fine ending.

Once The Great One started pulsing, they halted any more from entering it. Now people were popping up on the ramp in groups of three and four at a time.

Bolt and Bubba were watching for Brand's arrival, like when a plane lands and you're waiting for a loved one to de-board. First, a few come out, and then the groups become large. As time goes by, it becomes few again, and finally, the last one exit. But the person you're waiting for never shows up.

As the last few popped in and the structure was getting progressively more unstable, their hopes were fading. Finally, one last man popped on the ramp. He was a proven, seasoned warrior.

Bolt looked him in the eyes, almost yelling, "Were there any left alive?"

This warrior looked him back with a stare that Bubba will never forget and stated, "I wouldn't have come back if there was." This was the last man who made sure everyone else went before him. Bolt looked instantly weak with his head down, saying, "Sorry, sorry, sorry, thank you!" It now looked like Bolt was in shock. Bubba helped Bolt back to the command center and provided for him what they had provided when he was affected.

Roxanne realized that Brand's orders to Bubba saved both their lives. Like he knew it would all break down quickly, yet never tried to get away. Roxanne helped Bolt even though there was medical personnel they were busy with wounded soldiers.

Chapter 32

THE END OF BRAND

Now there was a change in The Great One. It stopped fluctuating and seemed whole again, but that did not last long. Then it started to shrink in all directions at the same time. Finally, ending in a dot that disappeared. It was gone, going from the 4th to the 3rd, then the 2nd and 1st dimensions. The only thing left was the empty space it had occupied. The threat had ended, and the world was safe again for now.

Roxanne tried to console Bubba regarding Brand, but Bubba would have none of it. He believed somehow, Brand was still alive. The crazy thing was Bolt acted the same way, saying Brand would show up, wait and see. Roxanne now wished she had gotten to know this man that other men believed could not be killed. The effect he had on people that are close to him was amazing.

The return trip seemed unreal, with Brand not being there for Bubba. They repeated the process just in reverse, with the submarine to the fishing vessel, then to the island, and then to the cargo plane. There is no sadder feeling than starting a trip and ending with less than all who began.

The people were very nice to him like they knew he had lost his best friend. Yet Bubba just could not believe Brand was really gone. It is the syndrome of not having a body. Without a body, how can you really know? All logic says one thing, but there is no body saying the other.

Three months had gone by with no Brand sightings or contact.

Nina asked Sam Smith, "Do you still want to hold off on the Dragonfly issue."

Sam not in a particularly good mood, responded firmly, "Yes."

Nina did not say what she was thinking, yet it seemed Sam picked up on it.

"Just say it."

Nina responded, "He's gone."

Sam looking sad replied without emotion, "You're dismissed." As Nina Woodhall was leaving his office, the heel on her shoe broke, causing her to fall on her back. Her elbow also got bruised on the fall down. It seemed unnatural, given the force of how fast she fell backward.

Sam instantly rushed to her, but she rejected his help, stating she was fine. Sam would never tell anyone that to him, it was a sign.

Colonel Bolt should have closed Subject 9's file months ago. He obviously perished in the pyramid as it collapsed into nothing. Still, he did not perform the finalization that is typically done when a subject has died. He was monitoring world events, but nothing out of the ordinary had happened. He expected there to be a bigger change when Subject 9 was gone.

Bubba never gave up hope on Brand's return. He remembered when Brand was lost in the wilderness. This was worse, but having true faith does not need logic. True faith in yourself or in a belief is quite powerful.

Chapter 33

DEBRIEFING

Nina received the call on the 96th day of Brand's disappearance.

"This is Allen Green. We have a 100% hit on John Doe 23. He is in New Jersey. Captured it from CCTV and confirmed with facial recognition. We have a team going to secure the situation. How would you like it to proceed."

Nina was caught off guard and had to go to her secure computer to look at the spreadsheet of who John Doe 23 was. The man she never expected to see again, Brand Wright.

"Pick him up and take him to-" and she gave Colonial Bolt's office address. Then she confirmed how long it would take till their arrival.

Now Nina contacted Bolt to inform him that Brand was alive and being taken to his office for debriefing. Then she contacted Sam Smith, who seemed not surprised to hear the news. In that regard, Bolt seemed happy but not surprised either.

Once Brand was finally at Bolt's office, which seemed like waiting for eternity to come. Nina decided she would attend the debriefing. It consisted of Bolt and Nina with Subject 9, Bolt sitting at his desk with Nina to his right. Subject 9 was in front of them both.

Bolt started with, "Congratulations on your successful mission, there are just a few questions, and you'll be home in short time." Brand just looked at him with a neutral state.

Bolt got right to the main question, "How did you get out of the pyramid, and why was it over three months before making contact?"

Brand now, looking at Nina and then at Bolt, said with amusement, "I don't think either of you have high enough clearance for that!" Then he added, "Guess it won't hurt, I have nothing to back up my story, and no one would readily believe it." Again he avoided telling the tale by looking at Nina and said, "You're Nina Woodhall yes?"

Nina responded by shaking her head up and down.

Brand, now getting serious, said, "I forgive you for trying to kill me, but only this once."

Nina was now looking white but said nothing.

Brand having everyone's full attention, continued, "I am surprised you want to be this close to me!"

Bolt now interjected to bring the mood back to friendly, "Sir, we all have great admiration for all you have done, and in this business, the past is just that. Please, if you could just provide us with the information asked, it would be appreciated."

Brand, now smiling again, "I will be glad to, but I also have some questions I would like answered. They are strictly about the last mission."

Bolt moved his head a little up and down and said, "Agreed."

Brand now started, "Major Lee was close to death, and I had an injury from my ankle to my hip. I could hardly move, so I stayed with the Major until he died. By then, the bodies were so many, and the structure was getting smaller, closing in on me. I was seconds away from the roof, crushing me when the Greys saved me. They used the light beam and transported me to their ship." Then smiling with a little laugh, "They broke the rules in doing that and fixing my body. Their time is slower than ours, and an hour is like a day in Earth time. After about 4 days, they beamed me to New Jersey. I have no idea why there. That's it."

Bolt had many questions, but Subject 9 would not be handled like an ordinary person. He thanked him, saying if we have any further questions, we will contact you. Thanks very much.

Brand did not move. He just looked at Bolt and asked, "How many died and how many were injured?"

Bolt now changed his manner to be much more official and answered, "The brave women and men were all volunteers, just like yourself. They gave their lives for their country and the planet. The First People had made many enemies, and if they reestablished their presence on this planet, they would have taken over humanity."

Brand had not moved an inch, just waiting. The silence was deafening.

Bolt then continued, "One hundred and eighty-three men and women were lost. Seventy-four were injured."

Brand looked fatigued, like someone being crushed by a weight too heavy to bear.

"Colonel Bolt, last year I made a vow to myself there would be no more blood on my hands. Even though I was not directly connected, people died around me. This year I have killed people with my own hand, and so many have perished because of being around me. I am in a sea of blood. Let me make this perfectly clear I am permanently retired."

Bolt understood how Subject 9 was feeling. It is a syndrome of war when you survive while so many fall. He compassionately said, "I understand. We have a car and driver to take you home or where ever you want to go."

Brand had the driver take him to Bubba's home. There he received a hero's welcome. To his surprise, Roxanne was there, yet they were very close during the mission. Bubba seemed more impressed that he had called it, that Brand was still alive.

Roxanne had a look of disbelief, she gave Brand a hug, but her affections were on Bubba.

Sweetbull went crazy and would not stop licking, leaning, following, and then repeating. She, like Bubba, knew he would be back. Animals had that type of instinct plus loyalty. A faith that doesn't need to have reasons. Brand and Sweetbull had a special connection.

He told the tale of how he escaped, but as he was finishing it, a sadness overtook his spirit. Sweetbull instantly picked up on it. It must have been apparent to all there as Bubba offered him the guest room for the night.

One hundred and eighty-three plus more with Hector's affair. So many gone connected to him. As he sat with Sweetbull in the very nice guest room, he felt he needed to make serious changes in his life. The solution in his mind was isolation. He would not be a complete hermit. There still would be Sweetbull and Bubba. But for everyone else's safety, that would be it.

PART 3

OFF TO MARS

Chapter 34

THE SEED

Forty-eight thousand four hundred square yards of space or more commonly known as 10 acres. Bubba had gifted Brand that amount of land to live on. Both men had been traumatized by the past events, just in different directions.

Brand wanted no more contact with people. That is why the gift of 10 acres was a joy to his heart. Nature has its rhythms. After a storm's destruction, there are no apologies given, no awkwardness, just part of the cycle. He started to hear and feel nature, seeing her beauty and how much life she supported.

The only downside was the problem that people with fame, power, or money have. In those cases, how do you know the people around you are there for you and not the other?

Brand now understood better his RB powers. Did he subconsciously influence Bubba's decision? The land was exactly what he wanted. How fortunate that Bubba gave it to him. Then again, Bubba was his best friend. He had also changed since their last adventure. Brand's changes were obtuse and easy to spot. Bubba's was subtle, yet if you knew him well could be seen.

Sam Smith and Colonel Bolt had become friends. For most, something normal that happens between people. These two men were made very much the same, having no friends or wives. Their lives revolved around their jobs with secrets that could be shared with no one. It is a lonely life. Loneliness draws itself to itself, maybe that was the cause of their friendship. Or it might be Subject 9, which Sam had an insatiable appetite for more information.

Bolt was talking about the simulation theory and how it can be seen by glitches in reality.

He then went deeper with, "So the glitches reveal the simulation, but what if there were only, say, 10 players out of 1,000 with all the other entities being computer-generated artificial intelligence with the freedom to make their own choices? How could you tell the difference between the real players and the AI-generated ones?"

Sam now pondered on the puzzle just described. "By their wealth, power, and positions?"

Bolt replied, "If the simulation was a game, then some real players would play well while others poorly. What if the real players had one advantage that the AIs didn't? This advantage being very subtle but still, a tell if you know what to look for. Exactly like what the RB program does. What if the real players can slightly modify the physics and other players around them? That would explain why so few have RB capabilities."

Sam now responded, "Interesting. On another issue, I want Subject 9 to pick up the Red Mercury and bring it back here."

Bolt now looking troubled, "Sam, I don't think that is wise. Subject 9 can be civil and then a killer within a second. He is totally unpredictable, which makes him dangerous. Now with Chameleon, he is a powerful force that really can't be controlled. The last time Subject 9 talked with me, he made it very clear he had permanently retired. He currently is isolated on 10 acres, and it's best to let it stay like that."

Sam, seemingly unmoved, responded, "Be creative."

Bolt, not backing down, "You know his profile. Without his willing participation, he will not comply with the mission at hand."

Sam nodded his head in agreement, "His friend Bubba likes adventures. Use him!"

Bolt understood what he was implying, and he was the boss. "Yes, sir."

Sam thought to himself, why would I let such a powerful asset rust in a field?

Manipulating people happens all the time. The only difference between the acts is how strongly it is implemented. All commercials, learning institutions, businesses, and governments use it.

One of the best and most subtle ways is to just plant a seed. Once planted, it will become the target's idea. Time is always a big variable using this method. Also, in who plants it, the higher the profile, the better its efficiency.

Bubba answered the call with, "Yea."

Bolt taken a bit back, replied, "Mr. Bubba, this is Colonial Bolt. We met once before. I am sure you remember."

Bubba now on full alert, "Yes, sir. What's up- what can I do for you?"

Bolt, feeling better, "Sir, I would like to take you out for lunch to thank you for your service. You were a big part of its success!"

Bubba had made a lot of money, but this was different. It was a feeling of national pride. Something that can't be bought except by earning it. He had never felt this type of emotion.

"Okay, that's fine. Where and when?"

Bolt provided the answers to those questions, with the last one being, should I contact Brand?

Bolt's response being, "Oh no, this is just for you. See you soon!"

Bubba arrived at a members-only fancy steakhouse and was seated on the reserved balcony. It had a beautiful view overlooking an area of sail and powerboats scattered across the water. The entire experience spoke power and privilege. Sure he could eat at expensive steakhouses if he wanted, just not this one. He noticed a few politicians and TV news personalities at other tables.

Bolt was already seated yet rose quickly to shake hands and thank Bubba for coming. After some informal talk and placing their orders, Bolt started to plant the seed.

"You and Brand are a great team. Have you ever been to Mars?"

Bubba feeling so good, did not really hear the question, answering with, "Oh yea."

Bolt smiling within himself, tried again, "My friend you have been to Mars?"

Now Bubba getting a little red, stammered, "Um no, you're talking about the planet, yes?"

"Yes, the Planet."

Bubba now thinking things through asked, "You want Brand and me to go to Mars?"

This was the critical part, where the real acting came in.

Bolt, like he just thought about it while getting a bit excited, "Well, we do have a package on Mars to be picked up and brought back here. It should be a piece of cake, and since Brand and you did so well before and you both have never been there, you will have memories for a lifetime-"

Bubba interrupted with, "We will do it, I have to talk to Brand, but I am sure he won't mind. It is just picking up a package and bringing it back, right?"

"Yes, that is all that is needed. It has to happen before Friday of next week. Just let me know. You have my number, and really thanks for all you have done for your country. We are really grateful for your service."

Bubba was so juiced up with excitement for the next mission to see Mars. Of course, he will have to have Brand go along. He would not think about going alone or with strangers. He was sure his good friend would appease him with this request.

Brand had given all the money he received from the last mission to St. Jude Children's Research Hospital. The money felt dirty, yet used for good would make it clean. Good always being for someone's benefit, just not his. So when Bubba gave him the 10 acres, it meant so much. It was like a dream that always seemed just a dream. Now a reality because of his good friend. That meant a lot, especially when Bubba asked for nothing in return.

There is a certain type of joy in pleasing people you love. A pleasure greater than pleasing oneself. More long-lasting and having no guilt, quite the opposite, it frees those burdens we carry. It is a gift that only can be given.

Brand also studied the habits of people. So when Bubba came unannounced, which was not his habit, Brand knew something was up. Sweetbull was the first to meet him, as she is usually the first in that regard, with a hero's welcome.

Being isolated from people makes the few you see that much more special. Brand was quite happy to see him and could tell some type of good news was coming. A lot of information can be obtained just from body movement. Bubba's strut and power of his stride implied he had important but good news to tell. Brand could see all that before his face came into view.

Bubba began, "How about a road trip to Mars?"

Brand playing along, "So how are we getting there?"

Bubba then looked perplexed and stated, "I never asked him that question, but Bolt said that we would have to go by the end of the week."

Brand now understanding much yet not wanting to kill his friend's excitement, "That's okay, I will just stop by his office and work out all the details."

Bubba looking a bit relieved, "Great, I thought you might not want to go, being your retired now."

Brand answered, "Bubba, you offer me a trip to Mars. Of course, we will go. I am as excited as you. Never been there!"

They talked some more, with Brand being extremely pleasant. It concluded that Brand would get back to him concerning all the details after his meeting with Bolt.

Chapter 35

A DEAL IS MADE

The atmosphere was strong candor, with two men who were not pulling punches. This not being their first meeting, it began with Brand in a cold voice saying, "Don't do that again!"

Bolt, who in the previous two meetings was very diplomatic, this time was different.

"Be more specific!"

Brand said in a strong voice, "Using Bubba to get to me and putting him in danger."

Bolt coldly said, "Every time Bubba gets into his truck, he is in danger. Being around you is dangerous! Next time I will be more direct. Are you doing it?"

Brand was going to go. He would not break his friend's dream. However, Bolt did not know that. There were some conditions to be met to make sure of the mission's success.

Brand began with, "What is the package to be moved."

Bolt, now going into his official mode, "You know I can't reveal that."

Brand fired back, "First, if I don't know what it is, how will I know if it is real or counterfeit? And without knowing, curiosity will just make me open it up. Obviously, it is something important cause I assume you don't just want to give

Bubba a ride to Mars. So important that sending in a team will just cause more problems. You know these things rarely go as planned. So what am I transporting?"

Bolt answered, "You won't be able to open it."

Brand said in a low evil voice, "You'd be surprised what I can do." That seemed to jolt Bolt into a different persona with a response much softer.

"Of course you're right. Have you heard of red mercury?"

Brand changing his mood completely replied, "I thought it was a hoax."

Bolt continued, "It's real but very elusive, almost impossible to make on Earth. Our scientists on Mars figured out how to create some, well, a very small amount. The only people in the know are the scientists who are quarantined, the security, and base commanders. You will meet with the security commander who will make the transfer, and then you will come back to Earth."

Brand now answering his next question, "And to get there, we take a Zero-G ship leaving from South America. Being below the equator, the ship is invisible to the Northern hemisphere. Am I right?"

Bolt was taken aback by the accuracy of Brand's statement. He questioned himself whether it was a guess or was this another ability not documented. Subject 9 was much more than just having RB capabilities. The real question was what they were and how powerful they could be.

Bolt answered, "You are correct."

Brand felt like he had taken control again and finished with his last request.

"How much cash for our daily expenses?"

Bolt seemed surprised, answering, "Converted to Earth's currency, Bubba, and you receive $5,000.00 a day, each. It is expected to last no longer than three days."

Brand, without seeming surprised or disappointed, countered, "Operations like this need plenty of money when dealing with unexpected events and unknown terrain. You know, if things go bad, the extra money might save the day. Make it $100,000.00 each, with it being converted back into Earth's currency and whatever is left, retained by Bubba and myself. I personally will not keep the money but have other plans for those funds. Do you agree?"

Now there was a silence that seemed to last quite long. In reality, it was 10 seconds when Brand interjected, "If I wait another 20 seconds, it will be half a million each and then 1 million after that." It was said very matter-of-factly, yet both men knew he would not back down.

Bolt's thoughts lasted another four seconds before he agreed to the terms. His thoughts went to how dangerous Subject 9 had become. Having Chameleon and RB powers would make anyone powerful, yet also having keen negotiation skills is like icing on the cake.

Chapter 36

THE JOURNEY BEGINS

Brand had a form of déjà vu. Even though he had never been on Mars or in space, the feeling that he was heading back to where he had left off was very strong. Those types of feelings are hard to describe and are fleeting in nature, making understanding them almost impossible.

Bubba was more excited than on his first mission to Antarctica. Brand also felt excited, yet he hid it from Bubba. This time they went on a standard airline to a place left undisclosed. From there, they were driven to another facility that was hard to see even when close by.

The building was more like a big rectangular basement having a very tall ceiling. There was a path off-center with ships on the left and right sides. It seemed like the bigger ships were to the left, with much smaller ships of sizes from 30 to 60 feet wide on the right. They were the classic saucer-shaped UFOs or what are now referred to as UAPs, Unexplained Aerial Phenomena.

After a short walk, they approached on the right a ship approximately 40 feet wide, having a circular shape. There were people already aboard, and as they got near it, the door opened, having stairs built into it. Then a ladder extended where the door had ended provided access to the craft.

Brand did not notice the door frame when approaching the ship. It seemed to just open from the solidness of where it was. That was only the beginning, for the ship was amazing. Brand tried to get as much information from the Captain about the ship as possible, which did not go well. The Captain had a secretive nature and was a loner by design.

Everything within the ship was curved, so no edges appeared, even when it came to the floor and walls. Most of the curves were subtle but still there. It was a testimony of engineering precision. Not needed for function yet showing how skillful the builder are. It had six passenger seats beside the captain and co-pilot chairs. There were two cabins, and in between them were the restroom facilities. The cabins also had private access to the restroom from either side of it.

There was a small kitchen that was built into the ship. The cabins, kitchen, and other facilities were around the back perimeter, leaving a large space where the passenger seats were located.

The captain stated that he would be staying on the ship when they arrived on Mars. This way, when Brand and Bubba were ready to leave, he would be there ready to go. He made it sound like if they needed to escape quickly at any time, he could handle it.

It was both reassuring and troubling at the same time.

Like a giant jigsaw puzzle, so big no one can see the real picture they create. Each group collected and organized its pieces. Moving them into place without the knowledge of the other groups. Yet all interacting to create something much greater than any could do on their own.

So forces were coming together that would change the structure of many other things not seemingly connected.

The entire trip was less than 4 hours. What information Brand could get out of the captain was to imagine a gyroscope. There was a magnetic field that surrounded the ship, and everything within this field was stabilized. The same way a gyroscope stays upright regardless of the movement around it. Not only were they stabilized from the velocity but also had an artificial gravity field surrounding them. It was less than earth's gravity but still kept you planted on the ship's floor.

The actual flight was uneventful. Even the landing was just like a freight elevator settling onto its desired floor.

Brand's first impressions of Mars were that of a large airport. They landed outside, and then the ship was moved to the docking port. From there, a makeshift tunnel was attached to the door, and they traveled through it and into the security checkpoint area.

It was a customs area plus, where they were questioned on where they came from, what their intentions were on Mars and how long they were planning to stay. They had brought their passports which seemed odd at the time but now was making perfect sense. Their bags were searched, and after some looks by the agents in charge, they were permitted entry.

Brand did most of the talking, giving the cover story that he was a galactic traveler and wanted to show his friend on Earth what Mars was like. They would be staying at most three days and then traveling to Jupiter's Moon IO to see the volcanoes. He would be staying at the hotel within the main Mars complex.

Once they exited the security section, there were huge windows connected to each other by the thinnest of joints, giving the illusion of one huge window providing a clear view of the planet Mars.

The sky was blue, a lighter shade than Earth's sky. There were no clouds to be seen, and the land had many different shades of color. In some areas, it was actually a shade of light green, with others being red dirt that reminded Brand of the Sedona region in Arizona. There were no roads, but Brand assumed that there were underground passageways to the major areas.

The building they were walking through did have some significant differences from buildings on Earth. Doorways were much taller, being a size of 20 feet high and 5 feet wide. The building itself seemed to use glass in many ways. The walls were a glass-like substance that could be clear or opaque while changing back and forth between states.

It was the other beings that had taken Bubba and Brand's full attention. There were many different life forms, and taking it all in without being overwhelmed was hard. Once you get used to things, and they can be really strange things, it is not a problem. It is getting used to part that takes time.

The pressure was on Brand to keep it together for Bubba's sake. It was a lot for Brand to handle, so he put on the attitude like this was all normal. He had seen some of the beings before, but there were some surprises. As he played that role, it started to feel natural to him.

There was a mini city within the structure they were in. Even if you went outside of the city's dome, which also was made of a very strong glass-like substance, there was breathable air. It was like breathing when you are at or over 10,000 feet elevation, thin but there.

As they looked at all the strange creatures, there were large and small Greys, of course, Martians and Earth people. Also, very pale beings that were 12 feet tall but looked frail. Small people that looked like hobbits. And what best can be described as Big Foot beings that were very large and hairy.

The amazing thing was everyone was getting along just fine. The signs were in many different languages, English being one of them.

Bubba was definitely having problems handling all of it. Brand was initially going to go straight to the Security Commander but figured it was better to get rooms and handle it tomorrow. After sleep and time, Bubba would be back to his old self and enjoying the new surroundings.

Many things were very similar to Earth with just slight modifications. There was a shuttle system underground similar to the monorail at Disney. Their Hotel was the 4th stop. The money system was very much like Earth. The cards they were given needed just the card and passcode for it to operate.

There were devices called vox, which was a voice translation device that would pick up the language spoken and feed the information into your head through a headband. If both parties were wearing the devices, it had a slight delay from hearing the first voice to the translation and then feeding it into your head. Yet it was very effective in communication with all the different species.

Also, the gravity on Mars was less than on Earth, making you feel stronger.

Brand realized that the patch he received from the First People was still working and having no problems doing translation across species. It also was quicker than the vox, yet he did not let on about having this ability.

When dealing in foreign lands, being more secretive is usually an advantage. They checked into their hotel rooms which were quite nice. The rooms were next to each other on the 3rd floor. There was a circular extension from the wall, which was the bedroom. The mattress was in the same shape as the circle, and there was a TV screen that was on the complete ceiling running down the walls leading to the bed. You could adjust the screen to view many different types of scenes. Not only was it a TV but also a holographic area where images within the bedroom area could be created.

One view was looking down on Mars like you were orbiting it from a ship in space. Another view was a snowstorm that felt very real, with snowflakes falling onto the bed. There were movies plus news to be seen and felt. Just experiencing that bed was worth the trip.

They ordered room service, which had a limited but wide selection of foods. Limited in the fact that most of the selections were unknown to both men. Being so new to the area, they kept their selections to what they were used to: burgers and french fries plus some sodas. At times it was hard to tell they were on Mars, except for the gravity always being less than on Earth.

Once the meal was done, they settled into getting some sleep. Then they would do the pickup and go home. That was the plan, yet often, plans never go as expected. Tomorrow would be no different.

Chapter 37

PROBLEMS ON MARS

To Nina Woodhall, it seemed lately she was always giving Sam Smith bad news. He was a very controlled man and had never been physical in doing her any harm. Yet just the act of telling someone so powerful things he does not want to hear, can always be dangerous.

He seemed to her different since the meeting with Dragonfly and Subject 9. Still, everyone has their breaking point, and she definitely did not want to see his. Once she was settled into a chair in his office, she began.

"Sir, the package at Mars was stolen just after Subject 9 arrived. He still is unaware of this development. We are looking into what happened and believe the security commander may be involved. What would you like done?"

Sam Smith was not an ordinary man. He had no special abilities, not the smartest nor strongest. He was the picture of ordinary, and yet the control of his thoughts was well above most people. To think a situation out with many probabilities in extreme detail in a short period of time. He was also a man who could be very short on words.

Sam seemingly not unhappy nor disappointed, said, "Nothing."

Nina now looking like she expected something else, anything else, responded with, "Yes, sir," and left his office.

Sam thought to himself, that is why I sent Subject 9 there. He is my solution to this foreseen problem. Then his thoughts returned to his replacement. Seems nobody was ready to meet the challenge.

The strangest thing about Mars is how similar it is to Earth. The Martian day is 24 hours, 39 minutes, and 35 seconds, so virtually no adjustments need to be made. The year is twice as long, minus two years, compared to Earth.

After a full 7 hours of sleep, which was preceded by over 18 hours of being awake, it makes you feel like a new person. Bubba and Brand ordered breakfast via room service, as the room itself was very pleasing. Also, Bubba was feeling much better, and not overdoing it with too much strangeness was part of the cure.

They worked their way back to the monorail, needing to get off at stop 6, which was where the Earth buildings were. From there, they walked to building 13. Bubba asked if Brand had contacted the person they were going to see. Brand responded that it was better to have fewer communications being you never know who is listening.

Bubba remembered now how important the mission was. Realizing that Brand always had a sense of security on his mind. It reminded him why old people were respected in the Wild West. Just the fact they were old said a lot. Bubba better realize how long Brand had been doing these types of things, how lucky plus wise he had to be.

They found the building, and after talking to a computer, well, actually arguing with it, Brand was told to wait for his interview.

Another computer came to lead them to the security commander, robotics being used quite extensively on the planet.

Hank was the name of the security commander who, when Brand and Bubba finally met, was having what is called a bad day. He looked annoyed and commanded them into a private room.

"Gentlemen, this way!"

Brand could already tell things were amiss by everyone around him, especially this Hank. The general feeling he was getting was Hank was annoyed having to be bothered by them. Now that Brand was retired and not worrying about a career, he had very little patience and could express much more freely how he felt.

They entered a small conference room, where Hank began with a bit of being sorry.

"Gentlemen, I have bad news. Your trip was for nothing. They stole the prize right before you arrived. Safe journeys home."

Brand could change emotions very quickly and now seemed angry, "You said they, so you at least know who has it! I want full details on exactly how it was contained and secured. How it was stolen and who has taken it."

Hank taken aback by Brand's attitude, "Who do you think you are? This is my base and I don't answer to you!"

Brand looking hard at Hank, taking many seconds before responding, "You realize you will be blamed for all of this. Don't you think there will be blowback? Do you think they just sent anyone? I am here trying to help you but have it your way. Have you seen Earth's prisons lately?"

Then with a smile, Brand looked at Bubba, saying, "There is nothing here to learn. It's time to enjoy Mars."

Now Hank feeling his power return, "You and your friend need to leave Mars by tonight, don't let me see you here tomorrow!"

Brand always had a temper, and as late, he cared not what it caused. They were all standing in front of the meeting table, which looked like it was made of some type of stone. It was definitely a heavy solid structure that was the pride of the room.

Brand tried again to convey to Hank, this time very softly and quietly, "Sir, I can help you. Do you know who sent me? Why are you pushing my help away?"

Hank still hype up with power and frustration demanded they leave Mars by night fall.

As they walked out of the room and then out of the building, Bubba asked, "Is it over? Are we heading back to Earth?"

Brand now with that smile which was a grin plus replied, "Over? Now it is just beginning, and no, we will head back to Earth once I know more."

Bubba, with a quizzical look, "How are we going to know more?"

Brand enjoying himself, responded more like he was talking to himself, "We go to the bars to find desperate people or people that like to gossip."

Nina Woodhall received the communication that the base commander on Mars wanted Brand Wright to return to Earth immediately. He threatened Hank, the security commander which should be addressed.

Nina contacted Sam to inform him of the current situation and find out what actions he wanted to take. After showing him the communication, she waited for his response.

Sam glazed over the communication. Then after what seemed like a long time, he said, "Subject 9 is doing exactly what I expected. Do nothing."

Nina now asks, "So what should I tell the base commander?"

Sam, from some far off place in his mind, answered, "Nothing, no response is necessary."

Chapter 38

ON THE HUNT

Mars was like a small town in that everyone knew everyone else's business. Most functions were automated, so the people that were left were few in number.

Bars may seem like places of happiness, yet loneliness pervades everywhere within those walls. All those who sit alone are just one sign. Other examples can be couples that have no interest in each other. They come in as one, but each looking for someone else's company. It does not stop there, with some having what everyone wants and still being terribly lonely.

There were many bars, some very small, with just a couple being full nightclubs. They started at one of the biggest, with Brand telling Bubba it may take some time. It was a process, and done right cannot be rushed.

The good news was that the card that their money resided on was more like a mini bank. It was set up to easily transfer money not just to businesses but to people around them. Besides a number pad for passcode entry, it also had a finger sensor for security. To transfer money with people around you, all you had to do was key in the amount on the number pad and then pick the type of transfer from the touchscreen and tap one card with the recipient card. Of course, there were many other ways of sending and receiving funds. For their purposes, it would be perfect. Now, all they needed was to find the right person.

It is hard to judge who really knows things and who doesn't. There are so many things you can't rely on, from fancy clothes to attitude. The old sayings sometimes are the truest. Brand was explaining all this to Bubba.

Brand continued, "Those who know do not speak. Those who speak do not know. It is finding the right person and prying the information needed. It may take one bar, or who knows. Either way, it should be a good time, so enjoy, my friend."

One of the main differences between Earth and Mars is the feeling that energy costs do not matter on Mars. There were moving sidewalks with lights that were always on. All the doors automatically opened and closed. Anything that could be accomplished with science and unlimited energy was infused together. All the moving Androids that surrounded them consistently, everything needed energy.

It was the fourth bar where they found their lead. Most would say she had used up all her good luck and now was living only with bad forces surrounding her. There was a beauty about her, but it only had remnants of its formal glory. Truly it was a great sadness for someone who was so young. Miranda was her name. She was sitting at the bar looking depressed but still trying to get a client for the night.

Brand sat down next to Miranda and said, "Maybe we can help each other. Do you know anything about the big robbery at building 13?"

Miranda acted at first like she didn't hear him, and then, "So all you want is info about that?"

Brand now getting more serious, "Real information that will lead me closer, yes, and I pay very well!"

Miranda turned her head, looking Brand in his eyes, "Yeah, I know a lot. How much you paying?"

Brand now smiling, "A lot, but it has to be real, meaning I have to feel like I am getting closer to recovering it. I need a story and a name. We go together to the name, and after an interview, I will pay you 10,000.00 Martian. But again, I have to feel like I am getting closer to it."

Miranda now fully awake, "For real, that is all I have to do?"

Brand just studied her face, her every expression.

"So what do you know, and where is this contact we are going to?"

Miranda starting to really come alive, "The talk is it was the Queen. Even if it wasn't, she would know what happened, but it was the Queen!"

Brand never taking his eyes off her, "Great, so let's meet the Queen."

Miranda laughed, "No one sees the Queen."

Brand, feeling he was being hustled, "So how do you know there is a Queen if no one sees her?"

"She's real. She has her own army!"

Brand's patience was already gone, as traveling to different bars throughout the night is not his form of pleasure.

"Well, Miss Miranda, let's go on a road trip to meet the Queen's army. After I speak with someone there, I will pay you."

With that, Bubba had gotten up, and Miranda, who must have felt it was all play-acting, saw that these two men were serious about seeing the Queen.

The three men looked like the rest in the bar. Two young men with one old man sitting and drinking. They keep their voices low when something changed.

The old man got excited, and literally started pumping his leg up and down. It was an unconscious tell that an important event had come.

He said, "That's CW. I am telling you that is him!"

Now the first young man replied, "You're drunk. I heard he was just a legend, completely made up. And even if he was real, his acts were exaggerated."

The old man would have none of it, "Get his picture quick. I think he is getting ready to leave!"

The young man moved quickly so he could get a good angle as Brand's group was closing in on getting to the exit door. The phones used by many in the Galaxy were a much better technology than those used on Earth. They had more global capabilities and used the standard technology used through-out the Galaxy. He got the picture and was shuffling back to his original group when he could hear the men arguing.

The second man kept saying that even if he was the same man, he was old, and the stories about him were blown up. What good could he be to the cause now? With that, the old man was livid, telling a story from the past.

"We were in an asteroid belt with rocks rearranging them-selves frequently. Had seven Corp ships coming up on our six with no shields or weapons. Life support was half working, but we still could drive her. The computer could not program a path quickly enough because of all the extra movement. CW jumped into the pilot's seat and, just off instinct, moved us through the belt. Only two Corp ships made it through that we had to deal with-"

The first man interrupted, saying, "Have your picture. What do you want done?"

The old man stated, "We need to contact her and find out what she wants done."

The first man looking troubled, "But you know there is supposed to be no contact until-"

The old man now interrupted him, "Do it. They will change their plan, you'll see. I take full responsibility, do it now!"

Sam Smith sent a message to Nina to have the Base and Security Commanders from Mars in his office at seven hundred hours tomorrow.

Miranda, Bubba, and Brand were headed to see the Queen. The reality was she had her own building, and anyone versed in Mars would know how to find it. They arrived at the building, which was easy, yet seeing the Queen was not happening, at least that is what her guard force insisted.

Miranda was getting fidgety and said she would take half the money offered if given right now so she could leave. She assured Brand quietly that the Queen had it. Maybe he was getting soft, or maybe she deserved trust and a break. Either way, Brand agreed and paid her the full 10,000 Martian.

Watching her eyes as she saw the full amount enter her account seemed to change her for the moment. A beautiful smile erupted, and some of the stress lines disappeared. She really had a beautiful innocent look.

She gave Brand a great hug, whispering thanks, with the last words being, "Be careful, love. They will kill you before you ever see her!"

Chapter 39

SEEING THE QUEEN

Brand conferenced with Bubba over their next actions. They were both tired, and the building would be there tomorrow after they had a good night's sleep. Then again, they were hot on the trail with a somewhat element of surprise.

It was agreed by both that getting some sleep and food while cleaning up from the drinking that had occurred prior would be the best course of action.

With that, tomorrow, they will see the queen. They traveled back to their hotel rooms. Moving around Mars was easy with the monorail and then moving walkways. The fact that the gravity effect was less than what they were used to made Brand feel younger than his age.

The three men were on a mission that involved stealth. The old man was right. It is CW, and communications from the Nevermore were very clear. All the plans would change, and retrieving CW became the only priority. They would have several hours before it was show time.

Ask anyone who has been called into the Principal's office, or the Boss's office expecting trouble coming their way. When Sam Smith calls you into his office, it's much worse than that.

That list included anyone Sam wanted to address, today being the two men working on Mars. His office had a private door that Nina had never seen opened before this day. She assumed it was a private den or something of that nature. Sam's office was large, and his desk very impressive. It's history was old like the creator knew it would be around for a long time. A big old desk gives the recipient behind it that feeling of going to be around a long time.

When the two men were seated, and Nina had taken her spot horizontally to Sam's location, but off to the side, the show began. Once the door to his office had shut, the other door within Sam's sanctuary opened.

Eight battle-seasoned warriors came into the room, women and men in full battle armor, with what weapons were seen being riffles, guns, and knives. Which were scary enough, yet there was a feeling in the air, an electric energy preceding imminent doom.

Nina Woodhall was now seeing another side of Sam not seen before. She was used to his coldness, yet now it seemed to invade his heart. The two men knew their lives were on the line. Nobody here was getting fired or going to prison.

Sam started with the security commander, "You lost the package and turned away the help that I sent. Explain yourself."

Hank was definitely flustered with having 22 eyes and ears watching and listening for his response.

He began poorly with his thoughts, not expecting this, "Well I- he tried to take command, ahh I was hard at work getting it back when he disrupted me. I could have-"

Sam showed signs of anger which was unusual for him, "Bag him!"

With that, four soldiers instantly surrounded the man, and as they pulled him up from the chair, he was handcuffed with hands behind his back, gagged, and a bag placed over his head.

He was then led by two soldiers to the private door they had entered through. There were two more soldiers on the other side, and the prisoner was led by the two soldiers who had been in the room.

Now there were six soldiers, Sam and Nina, plus the base commander.

Sam now looked at him and said, "You were in charge, and have let us down. What do you have to say?"

The man, without hesitation, stated, "I can still help your man. If you let me return to Mars, I will do all I can to benefit him. I can still make a difference!"

Sam gave him one of his long looks, "Make that difference!"

Then the soldiers all left the room via their private entrance with just Sam, Nina, and the base commander.

The base commander then said, "Sir, may I leave now? I want to get back to Mars. I will make a difference, please?"

Sam, already in some other place within his mind, shook his head up and down and motioned with his hand he could depart.

Nina was troubled by the whole episode. First, was Subject 9 somehow influencing Sam? Subject 9 had a dislike for Hank, the security commander, and now he was going to die per Sam's hand. Second, now the base commander was determined to help Subject 9 in any way he could. Again helping Subject 9, was this just Sam's actions, or was he somehow being influenced?

That is the real problem with Subject 9. He gets into your head and makes you question things that would have never been questioned before, once you truly understand his powers.

Brand had a gut sense that he was on the right track. The sense was also saying it won't be easy to see the Queen, but it is imperative.

There is nothing like a good night's sleep, which both men had. Now, after a quick breakfast, they were ready to meet the Queen. Brand suggested Bubba go back to the ship. That there was a great chance of violence, and he would feel better knowing Bubba was safe.

Bubba was a strange man. He had so much that so many would love to have. Ninety-nine percent of people with his resources would run to that safe ship. The trip was already a success for Bubba. He had flown to Mars, and been on a different planet than his home world. Having stories, he knew no one would believe but still wanted to tell. Everything to gain by going back to the safe ship.

Bubba responded with a shrug, "You ready to go?"

It was not hard to find the Queen's building. It had not moved from the night before. There was a reception desk fitted with hard-looking creatures having human characteristics yet different. Their height was about 8 to 9 feet tall with thick wide bodies. They only had three fingers and a thumb, yet they were huge, and the fingers and thumb spaced like a human hand. Their heads were large, but their eyes little and very forward on their face.

It is easy to be intimidated by creatures bigger and stronger than yourself. Especially when they are so ugly and could very possibly mean you harm.

They were not wearing any voxes yet could speak and understand English. It is always a sign of intelligence when beings can speak multiple languages without the help of computers. These creatures were smart and needed to be treated with respect.

As usual, Brand wanted to do the talking, which right now was fine with Bubba.

Brand started with, "Good morning. I would like to see the Queen."

His name was Utago who replied, "Go away!"

Brand, seemingly not deterred, "Why don't you let her know I am here? I am sure she will want to speak with me."

Utago now looked up and into Brand's face, "I told you, go away. Do you want trouble?"

There were four of these creatures, but only Utago spoke while the others watched intently.

Brand acting like they were just reminiscing about old times, "Well, if dying is the only way to get her attention, so sorry to have to kill you."

It seemed obvious to Bubba that Brand was trying to get Utago upset, and it was working to perfection. The real question is what comes next. Brand and Bubba both had guns. Weapons with projectiles are frowned upon on Mars. If you use an energy weapon, there is much less blood to clean up, and it is safer for everyone near the event.

Now Utago rose from the chair behind the table. His full height and power showed. He was young, trying to make a name for himself in the Galaxy.

He walked around the table and was now sorta facing Brand. He was looking down on him and with a movement that was unbelievably fast, especially for his size. His hand just snapped on Brand's chest, and he went flying backward. Luckily there was a padded bench seat, for that is what stopped Brand. Then the bench moved another 4 feet back before resting in the new spot.

It all happened so fast that Bubba could only react after the bench and Brand had stopped. He went running over to his friend to inspect the damage inflicted.

Utago was just amused at how weak the human was. He was now ready to kill him and pulled out his weapon, which fired electrical pulses that looked like light balls. This type of weapon was favored by many in the galaxy, with just different variations of the same technology used.

At that moment, an old man shouted out, "Cover CW!" Then he started to shoot at Utago with a weapon very similar to Utago's weapon. It can shoot an electrical charge so great it could sever your arm, and there would be no blood depending on how wide you set the blast and intensity levels, which creates different types of damages. The wider the blast setting, the less damage done with greater chance of hitting the target. That was the setting the old man had when he fired upon Utago.

The old man did hit Utago, but it did not kill him. The next moment the old man was dead. During that brief time, two younger men were running over to the area where Brand and Bubba were at. One man got in front of Brand and Bubba, while the second man was 8 feet from him. He was shooting at the three other guards, who were all shooting back. He had caused a distraction giving Brand's group vital time needed to get to a safer position.

It looked bad as Brand was still having trouble moving, and five more Queen's guards came into the room.

Just when it seemed the end was moments away, ten men from the Mars police force stormed into the room. Five went over to Brand, Bubba, and the unknown man. His friend had been killed just seconds before. Then everyone was firing at the Queen's guards. By firing in two directions, they had pinned down the guards with no more being able to enter the room.

Chapter 40

FINDING RED MERCURY

It had turned into a temporary stalemate when the Martian Police Chief reached Brand's group, which was now pushed far away from where the action was. He said he had the Queen on the phone, and she would allow just you and Bubba to see her. He advised against going in alone without his men to provide protection. In reality, the Queen was just a title she had assumed and her men just bodyguards.

To Brand the fact that the Queen would see him and Bubba was all that mattered. In the back of his mind, it seemed odd she would mention Bubba. On the other hand, they had traveled to Mars together.

Brand told the Martian Police Chief that he accepted the Queen's offer and Bubba and himself would be fine. With that, the man spoke into his phone, and all the Queen's guards retreated. Then a wall started to move, and behind it was a grand staircase that you would see in the old movies.

The Chief again advised against going alone, but Bubba and Brand just wanted to get it over with by this point. Brand had a gut feeling that it would be safe, and Bubba showed no fear.

They traveled up the stairs that were quite wide, being 10 feet plus as they expanded in length the higher up they went. Its banisters were intricate metalwork with wood railings.

Once they arrived at the top, there was a parlor room and, beyond that, a secret secure den. The Queen liked many moving walls, and it was hard to tell the real dimensions of her rooms. The secret den was revealed when another wall slid out of the way.

This den was very secure and could withstand a huge onslaught if required. By the nature of someone who would design a den like this, there would also be an escape chamber.

Still, they had not met the Queen. After they arrived at the top, the walls kept opening, and they just followed into the new rooms. Now the Queen was ready to make her entrance.

She was even more beautiful than the last time Brand had seen her.

Bubba said in disbelief, "Well, if it isn't Miss Joy!"

Dragonfly just smiled with that sweet smile, "Mr. Bubba, what are you doing on Mars?"

Brand jumped in, "Well, we were going to IO for the volcanos just thought we would stop here at Mars since we were already out."

Dragonfly, with less sweetness said to Brand, "So you thought to stop by and say hello? How kind of you."

Brand now felt like something bigger than what just went down was coming. It made him feel like he had a short time to achieve what was now needed. Really it could not be described, just a feeling, not even a vibration. More like a thought that felt more than just a thought.

Brand now getting down to business with Dragonfly, "I am here for the red mercury. Not all of it. Just enough so I don't go back and feel guilty."

Dragonfly looked into Brand's eyes and said, "I was seconds away from making Sam Smith pay for his crimes and you ruined that. I knew that you were lying at the meeting. Now you come into my domain demanding my red mercury! I should kill you instantly without a thought or care. Yet your boldness and the fact that in ways we are so much the same, makes us kindred spirits. It is fate that you are here right now. For something wonderful is going to happen, and I will share it with you and Bubba."

After she said all that, there was silence in the room. When giving a speech, you know you made real contact with your audience when they are speechless. Now with a youthful sweetness, she spun around and hit some holographic keypad, and another small wall swung open. There was a small room that looked like a mad chemist was trying to create something that needed 100 tubes.

It was a very complex setup with tubes going from one area to another, all having bottles and other types of containers. Some had heat applied while others were being stored in a chill state. It all led to one final vessel that held a liquid appearing to be of a whitish sparkling color.

There also was a giant digital clock with the numbers being 3 feet tall. It was ticking down by seconds and then minutes with 8 minutes and 23 seconds showing.

Dragonfly looked at Brand and asked, "Do you know about the philosopher's stone?"

Brand, now thinking that it is odd that within one week, he was asked about two things he believed were myths.

"Yes, but never believed it was real."

Bubba now barged in on the conversation, "Guys, little help here!" He said with a big smile.

Brand and Dragonfly looked at each other with Brand responding, "Well, the short version I know is that it can change metals into gold. Also that a formula can be created with it to extend life." As he finished with his last statement, he looked into the room with the vessel of liquid. The clock was now to 7 minutes and 13 seconds.

Brand looked at Dragonfly while asking, "The clock countdown. Is it what I think it is?"

Dragonfly, now looking a bit stressed, answered, "Yes. Excuse me, but I have some cooking to do."

With that, she pulled out three shot glasses and began to mix three potions of extending life. Even if she had the right substances, it is not known if she had mixed them properly. Yet when you are one of the smartest people on Earth and Mars, the odds are better than not she got it right.

After it was mixed and waiting in three shot glasses, she started to explain the clock.

"Now I know you just want to drink it now. Time is a crucial factor in its working. Once the clock gets down to zero, it must be taken right then with no delay. We will share this experience together." As Dragonfly said this, there was a feeling in the air of friendship and trust. All three were now looking at the clock, which was showing 4 minutes and 23 seconds.

Chapter 41

THE NEVERMORE

When she was created, she was the flagship of the fleet. Her official name was Mercy, yet she had more firepower than any other ship they had. Her crew was the best the SSP had to offer. Of course, the Secret Space Program wasn't very secret.

After 30 years, most of the original crew was gone, and her systems had been retrofitted to the latest technologies. Yet she had a spirit that lasted long after she unofficially had her name changed.

Their current mission was a retrieval, not just any pickup, one that would change the war. They had called in every favor currently they had. The attack would be strong on either end of the complex with a stealth mission to attain the goal. The target was located almost dead center of the complex. With all the action being on either side of where they were heading to, they expected little resistance.

Even with their plans, they brought more than what would be expected, no surprises, was the motto. These people had been fighting the war for decades. Some, for their entire lives, they were hardened and disciplined, plus very focused.

They had broken stealth mode and were now in conversation with the agents on the planet. Their assignment had been to shadow the prize and assisted if needed on capture.

There was a lot of energy on the bridge, with many crafts moving around the area. You could feel that plans were being made, other plans going into effect. Each player making moves regardless of the other players around them.

Their ship was committed to its position and task. Most wondering why they haven't begun the attack already. The general feeling is that the longer they delay, the worse their chances will get. They waited for the command.

The Martian Base Commander was no fool. Times as he had just been through needed thinking on your feet. First, he contacted Mars and had them send a team ready to help if needed for the two new arrivals. Later he heard that there was some action, but Sam's people were still alive, and it was currently in truce mode.

In a way, this was perfect cause it proved he had helped. If that wasn't enough, another problem was conveyed that was troubling. The information was that Mars was going to be attacked, and from how many ships are around its space, it would be extreme.

He instructed to have all their ship flying, and also he was going to contact SSP and GF for reinforcements. The only problem is everything takes time.

Galaxy Corporation was an anomaly that was bound to happen. The corporation started by moving goods from all over the Galaxy to other parts. They were able to move vast amounts quicker than the established means prior to their creation. Folding space is a popular way of moving around the galaxy. Galaxy Corporation was able to do multiple space folds without the wait that is usually needed between jumps.

The variety of items plus others being able to sell through them created growth unseen before. Between low prices and speed of delivery, they were loved by their customers.

To some, that may have been enough, but it was just the start for Galaxy Corporation. They moved into services supplying the Galaxy with easy access to so many different needs. Then into media, all forms. They created multiple types, from social to a world database.

Of course, they would need their own protection force, which was called Galaxy Force. The best trained and well-supplied military that has ever been assembled. Their force against any one world's strength would be no battle, just destruction of that world or its people.

GC as it is known to all, lastly got into the government business. It had an immediate advantage, no taxes. Between all the income it made through sales and services, it could supply a complete government infrastructure with a police force for no charge to the citizens it governs.

Also, it prided itself on being honest. No bribes or corruption is tolerated within their government division. Everything was done internally with no real interaction with the public, and GC was its own government with very strict laws and consequences.

Also, the populations that accepted their leadership received special discounts on different items and services.

Needless to say, they very quickly became the official government of the Galaxy and many of the planets within.

Like most things, there were pockets of resistance. Planets having reasons for not wanting to be dependent on GC. Once all their goods and services were available, it was very hard not to keep using or needing them. Like any dependency, it becomes stronger as time continues.

There were planets because of feuds, or their religious natures would not be customers of GC. Yet there were so many that used GC its power and resources seemed to be unlimited.

GC was the most diversified organization the Galaxy had ever seen, yet the real control was handled by a very small centralized group that numbered less than six members called The Core.

The war started as just a raid on a supply station. There will always be that type of thing, and it was not registered as any real concern to the people immediately in charge nor The Core.

In hindsight, there were differences between the attacks. They were organized and executed with military precision. Even more than that were the targets chosen and the aftermath of the people affected.

The raiders would give most of the items taken to the people living there. They became a modern Robin Hood. The general population of these planets protecting them, plus giving them hero status.

Even worse than that were the copycats that followed their lead. No matter how many copycats were destroyed, as long as the ship that began this was out there, no peace could be had.

Nevermore was the ship's name and as far as GC was concerned, destroying her was the top priority.

There was one person even worse than the Nevermore, which they had assigned a special name to. He was called Plutoneus, for they were the type of people to give honor even to their most hated enemy.

They had made a deal that he would have his memories wiped and be stuck on Earth until his natural death. As much as they hated him, they also respected what he had created. Somehow he challenged the greatest might in the Galaxy, leaving a small revolution in his wake.

Chapter 42

TIME

Nina was telling Sam about the deteriorating situation regarding Mars.

"Sir, we believe Mars will be attacked very shortly. Do you want ships sent there?"

Sam looking very distant and tired, replied, "No."

Nina feeling troubled, "Do you want Subject 9 to return immediately?"

Now Sam awoke from deep thought, "Absolutely not!"

Nina could sense something else was going on, something big, so she pressed the issue. "Sir, what is really happening? Please, totally off the record."

Sam really liked Nina. She was loyal and a hard worker, plus smart and attractive. He responded with, "A very large war is going on in the Galaxy, and Subject 9 is a big part of it."

Nina asked in amazement, "You started a war?"

Sam had that look he had often now, more sadness and disappointment than anger. "No Subject 9 started the war 30 years ago. I just reactivated it."

Vision is a combination of perspective and scale. Take Earth and the billions of people that live there. One hundred years ago, it would seem impossible to have the amount of information that is available on each person living there. Now imagine instead of people, worlds.

The Core had agents on each world that collected information the way governments on Earth collect information from their citizens. Then the millions of worlds with billions of citizens are collated and analyzed with algorithms and other filters. The final result is minuscule information can rise from the huge amounts collected.

The Core was already aware of the Nevermore being in the region of Mars. The Nevermore was fast and dangerous and had tried to be captured or destroyed many times before. They were working on new plans for its current destruction when something even bigger than that was brought to their attention.

Plutoneus was not on Earth, and not only that but was extremely close to the Nevermore. Plutoneus was on Mars, and even worse than that, the Nevermore and Plutoneus must never be reunited.

This information was brought to The Core for their commands.

As Brand watched the clock tick down, now to 3 minutes and 22 seconds left before they would all drink for extra life. He wondered why he even wanted more time. When you're young, of course, you want a long life. Assuming that it will be filled with good times, if not at least interesting or exciting events.

Once a family is started, you have to be there for them if not for yourself. Once you reach the late years, unless there is a major project at hand, the desire starts to fade. There always is the just want to see one more day, yet even that ends.

Between the pain and loneliness, it is a hard road to bear. Now looking at Bubba, who was still young, just entering his early 40s, and Dragonfly, who was 35 but looked more like 25. Yes, for them, it made perfect sense.

Brand was a different story, with his looks already gone and pain from so many different areas, what really is the point? He looked again, and there were 2 minutes and 32 seconds left.

The secret space program, which everyone in the know knew about, had a personal grudge against the ship called the Nevermore. It was their flagship, the best of the best crew, and they turned renegade. Becoming a Ronin like in feudal Japan or in modern times, what would be called a free agent.

They had also heard about reports that the base on Mars was going to be attacked. People involved in the SSP were military and scientists, with the military being the bulk of their force. They were born to be in battles, this one having a real reason for victory.

It was not like the Nevermore was needed or even current. It just was the principle and battle that mattered, even though 25 years of disobedience is not really long in the scope of things. What is important is that it will be terminated. Then it will become another footnote in military history.

They sent everyone they had to intercept. Being the ships were in different locations with varied speeds of travel, they would not all arrive at the same time.

The Core were not impulsive beings, and with all the success they had, who would argue with their commands. They ordered all their superships, which could destroy whole planets, that were within 10 sectors to go to Mars. Also, they ordered their elite ships within 20 sectors to that area. All were sent on high alert to start the genocide on everyone within the space and land of Mars upon their signal.

This was unexpected by them as they liked to be more surgical in their attacks. It was determined in this case the danger was too great to do anything except a massive destruction of everything.

Truth was, it wasn't the danger as much as being able to destroy Plutoneus. This might be their last chance before he dies of old age. Then there could be no glory, no real joy in knowing he defeated them without true punishment.

To the Mars' base commander, he was surprised at how quickly and easily GF and SSP agreed to send help to Mars. They assured him they would send all the support they could muster and just hold on a bit longer until their full force arrived.

He thought they might want to negotiate a fee upfront, yet neither party did. It was like the stars were all aligned for his benefit. He should be arriving in about 22 minutes, and then he could direct events from his office.

Dragonfly was now getting messages on her phone and other devices that seemed ominous. She kept her eyes on the clock, which was now closing in on under 2 minutes. Brand also was watching the clock closely.

There is a special beauty in innocents. Bubba was blissfully unaware of how in peril they all were. He was just enjoying himself. Occasionally looking in the direction of the clock. He was more into his own thoughts than what was happening around him.

The Nevermore was not alone. The reality was Mars space was getting so crowded that even if the ships didn't start shooting, they would soon just accidentally crash into each other. They were all there, and more were coming to the party each moment.

Yet all the ships seemed to be waiting for their orders to begin. So they all just floated around waiting, waiting for someone to start shooting.

Quantum computers prove that parallel universes exist. That is how they work by going into many other universes, each working on the problem and then coming back with the results. This is all happening at the same time.

The Nevermore had its own, which was set to determine the best possible future outcomes for a given event in this universe. This raid on Mars was just a normal one, but they always do extensive planning. They had been planning this mission for two months. Their Quantum computer provided suggestions to create the best future outcome.

It was surprising even to the hardcore believers how many "other" ships showed up for support. The message was sent out three weeks earlier to show up here and now, and they did!

Given the nature of time, the future is just different probabilities, with the strongest usually occurring. It truly is not defined the way the past and present are. There were six recommendations, but the top two were as follows. First was to gather as many reinforcements as possible, for they might very well be needed. The second was to hold off on the attack for as long as possible before engagement.

Now the commander of the Nevermore felt the time was right to attack. It would start on either side of the target, with an elite team sent in for retrieval. He signaled to send the communications for the show to begin.

Chapter 43

THE ATTACK

As the clock moved closer to zero, the three participants sat in a triangle orientation to each other. Brand had a perfect and constant view of the big clock. For a long time in the past, he kept seeing the number 111.

Now the big clock was approaching those digits. Maybe it was an impulse or a premonition, or just for dramatic effect. Whatever the cause, it startled Dragonfly and Bubba.

As the clock numbers displayed 1:11, Brand picked up his glass and, with one gulp, drank it until it was completely finished. Bubba and Dragonfly just looked at him with wide, questioning eyes. All Brand could do was give them that look like when you're young and do something stupid you can't explain.

Dragonfly was just starting to talk when there was a blast outside the door so strong it created a shock wave that moved everything in the room that wasn't locked down. The other two glasses were gone, and their ears were not working properly. After about 20 seconds, things started to resume regarding their hearing. The door had been breached somewhat. It was still standing, but there was a gap showing the outer room.

From their perspective, it seemed like the entire Mars base was under attack.

Dragonfly regained her senses first and opened a desk drawer. She pulled out three air masks which looked like one-inch thick face masks you would see on Earth. They were somewhat firm but fit securely over the nose and mouth.

Dragonfly said, "If we lose total air, these will last about 30 minutes. Other than that, they will help for quite a while." Then she looked at Brand with a bittersweet smile and said, "You're amazing. Two days on Mars, and look what you have done. We both know they are after you!"

"I am sorry about this," he said, moving his arms in a sweeping motion. "I feel you're right, but I really don't know why. I need you to take Bubba back to Earth."

Bubba was now getting that mad look and was just about to say something when Dragonfly looked firmly into his eyes and said.

"Dear Bubba, you need to trust your friend. He is trying to protect you and Earth! They are destroying Mars just to get him, and they're also sending a message to the Galaxy. I will explain it all to you once we're on my ship." Then she said very quietly to him, "Bubba, you know how he is. They will be lucky if they survive once he is with them. We will take the long way home." With that, she gave her smile, which is irresistible in not obeying her commands.

Dragonfly then went over to Brand and gave him a hug, whispered something in his ear, and what seemed like a little kiss on his neck. Turning again to Bubba, she said, "Come on, love, it's time to go." With that, she headed to a corner of the room. There she activated what turned out to be an escape hatch leading them down to her main ship waiting below.

The problem with chaos is that when everybody is doing their own agenda, eventually, collisions occur, especially when there is no need for it to happen at all. The new security commander of Mars, after talking with the base commander, decided on his own to capture Brand. He was not ordered to do that, just thought it would be a good idea.

The last person Brand expected at the door, as it was being pried opened, was Miranda. There she was with a face full of fear.

She started pleading, "You need to give yourself up, or they will kill me!"

Brand, without hesitation, shouted, "I give up! Please, don't hurt her!"

Now the door was opened enough for Miranda, the security commander, and his men, which accounted for six more people to enter the room.

The security commander stated to Brand, "You don't need that air mask. The dome in this section is not under attack. We still have LS working. I want you to put these handcuffs on. They're very special." As he said the last part, there was a cruel smile on his face.

Again Brand, without hesitation, put the handcuffs on with his hands being bound in front of his body. At that point, the security commander seemed to relax a bit and began talking again.

"You're not very smart!" With that, he shot Miranda in the back while looking directly at Brand.

The sound of the weapon's blast changed everything. To Brand, Miranda was a good person, the poster child for someone just needing a second chance. She still had so many possibilities before her. Like innocence lost, a sad short story that deserved more of everything. More love and definitely more time.

The rage he felt was quick and immense. It was as if time had stopped, for nothing seemed to be moving, and he could hear no sounds.

At that same moment, they all were now under attack from a group that was using sharpshooter tactics. First, two of the six went down, and then another man fell to the floor. At that point, all attention left Brand, trying to find out what was happening.

It's an old rule, a major rule that is wise to follow, never take your eyes off your enemy, and definitely never expose your back! The man who had just killed Miranda now turned to see what was happening behind him. This left his back exposed to Brand, and his two men left in front of him. They were being picked off one at a time by an unseen enemy.

Brand kicked the back of the man's knee, causing him to go forward on both his knees. Then Brand punches him on the head while looking for a weapon. His hands were still cuffed, but he saw what looked like a paperweight or half brick.

Once he had his weapon, he kept pounding the man's head. First, he felt the skull break then he started to feel the blood and brains.

It was then that he whispered into his dead ear, "She was innocent, unlike you and me." With that, he continued to bash his bloody dead skull.

"Sir! Sir! Sir! CW, sir! CW" The man in charge of his rescue party was trying to make contact with Brand. He had a wild eye kill look in his eyes with no one wanting to get close.

"Sir, we have to go. Time is running out. Sir, CW, please! We have to leave!"

Bubba had never seen a ship like Dragonfly had. For that matter, most people hadn't. Her ship was huge, being over 300 feet in diameter. It was designed like a luxurious personalized yacht, with fine marble floors and granite countertops. It had all types of exotic materials, forming a palace in space. With ships like that, their weight had no meaning since it had control over gravity around it.

Dragonfly had given some commands, and they did a jump to a totally different part of space. Millions of light years away where there were no ships to be seen nor planet below. In reality, no matter how fast light appears to people on planets when traveling through space, it is extremely slow. Even if a ship could travel at the speed of light, what good is it when the two points may be 40,000 light-years away? Who has 40,000 years to get there?

Dragonfly was now with Bubba, trying to explain all his questions. She could tell he was troubled leaving his friend behind, so she started with this statement.

"Dear Bubba, we know him as Brand Wright, yet he has many names. He is called Plutoneus by the Galaxy Corp and also called CW by the Nevermore. The Council of Nine calls him one of the Chosen, and U.S. Government calls him Subject 9. And I am sure he will have more names before his time is done. He is special and has a history most will never know. He started a Galactic war three decades ago, and people are still fighting it long after he left.

He is drawn to adventures like the hand of fate that leads him there. I know about the pyramid adventure you and he had recently. Let me ask you one question, did he seem nervous, or was he enjoying himself?"

Bubba had not said a word, just listening and thinking, then he responded.

"He was enjoying himself."

Dragonfly continued, but with a bit of sadness in her voice, "We all had a chance of prolonged, extended life. It was sitting there in front of the three of us, and who ended up receiving that gift? He has an uncanny ability to win when others around him lose."

Now Bubba jumped in, "How much longer will he live with that stuff you created?"

Dragonfly's answer was very vague, "It's hard to tell, he had taken it earlier than he should, and there are so many other variables to consider. Anywhere from 10 to 1, maybe 20 to 1, he will definitely outlive us.

Bubba now said, "10 to 1. I am not sure I understand?"

Dragonfly put on a smile saying for every ten years that goes by, he will age one year. But it might be longer than that. I went to Mars just for the Red Mercury. I had the formula for the philosopher's stone, and you know the rest."

Now Bubba seemed a bit sad, realizing how close he came to that gift. Being on Dragonfly's amazing ship brought him back to his usual self in a short time. There were so many unique items he had never seen. Just the beauty of the vessel was awe-inspiring

Then Bubba asked, "How did he start a Galactic war?"

Dragonfly began to tell the story, "He was commanding the ship called Mercy-" with that, she smiled to herself and continued, "There was a planet in desperate need of a vaccine which was in plentiful supply on another planet very local to the planet in need. The problem was they did not have the money to buy it. Brand rebelled against the SSP and renamed his ship the Nevermore. He then began a mercy mission stealing the medical supplies and giving them to the planets in need. He became a modern Robin Hood and continued doing missions of similar nature. The Galaxy Corporation, or GC, and the Nevermore were now in a war with the Nevermore always one step ahead of GC.

He was betrayed by his closest friend. They had his memory of those last ten years wiped, and he was exiled permanently to Earth. But the Nevermore never went away, and there were many ships that followed in its lead. No matter how hard GC tried to eliminate the problem, it still remains active.

Once GC realized he was on Mars, the truce ended, and now Earth is in peril. That was the deal. As long as Brand stayed on Earth, the planet was spared any trouble from GC."

Now Bubba's mind was exploding with questions.

Dragonfly, looking concerned, said, "Mr. Bubba, I suggest you get some food and sleep, and we will talk tomorrow. I will show you your cabin." With a big smile and hand extending, she led Bubba to his domain.

Chapter 44

BOXED IN

Sam Smith didn't like Galaxy Corporation. Once you become involved with them, they eventually take control of everything. With GC, you are always the pebble, and they are the pond. Of course, there were many reasons to welcome a group like that, but the cost is always power and control.

He felt they would take over Earth militarily or economically once their Subject 9 died through natural or unnatural causes. Yet, with Subject 9 at the height of his powers, could the unbelievable happen? Starting a war, a big war, that will involve many people and planets, is serious business. The question is, can Subject 9 meet the challenge of defeating the most powerful organization the Galaxy has ever seen?

Brand had finally come back to normal, yet now they were pinned in their position. There was the Galaxy Force of soldiers attacking both the front and back entrances. The team commander in charge of Brand's extraction was in communications with the Nevermore.

Mars's security force had withdrawn from the battle, and the SSP forces also were not taking either side between Brand's group and Galaxy soldiers fighting. There were fighters not part of the Nevermore that were helping Brand's group. You could tell by their lack of equipment and clothes. Their determination and bravery were impressive while providing enough support so that the extraction team was not overwhelmed.

The situation was not tenable, with the building and Brand's group in imminent danger. Team commander ordered everyone to put on their air masks which were similar to what Dragonfly had, with the plan being that the Nevermore would break the dome enclosing that area of the base. The distraction hopefully will allow their group to exit the back and reach a shuttle ship to the Nevermore.

It reminded Brand of the many plans he had like that when working in the field. A general outline yet to meet the conundrums of what is to follow. It was something, and remaining there was not an option.

They moved to the ground level, which was a battle in itself, and finally reached the back exit of the building. The structure of the building was that the front and back doors were on the same side and to the left of the building, unlike most buildings where the door is centered in relation to its design.

This gave the Galaxy forces an advantage since they only needed to cover one side of the building. They had a large group at the front door with a bit smaller assembly at the back door, even with the smaller assembly Brand's group was still badly outnumbered.

It seemed like an impossible task, getting out the back door and to the shuttle ship. They were going to use a tank formation with Brand in the center. Hopefully, they would get him to the shuttle before all were killed. That would be the best scenario. If Brand dies before that, all would be in vain.

Events happening outside the building had settled down for the moment with everyone taking their positions and just the occasional firing of weapons. It felt like the center of the storm, a peace that was anxious to break into madness, just impatiently waiting.

The sound of the air escaping the dome started with a pop, then a low sound gaining volume until it reached a steady level. It reminded Brand of when he went in a three person submarine to the depths of 900 feet. After they arrived back to the surface and the hatch was opened, the rushing air from the submarine to the outside world was very similar, just shorter and quieter.

Brand's imagination thought people might be flying upward into space like people in a plane when the cabin pressure has been breached. It did not happen that way with all the people being fine. Almost everyone there had some form of an air mask. There were definitely different style yet all having the same basic function.

Once the dome had been destroyed, it just felt right to try to escape. The mood was grim as there were just too many of the enemy. Even with Brand in the middle, there was a chance none of them may make it to the shuttle.

They assembled into position, and as they opened the door, immediately, there was a commotion happening.

The Secret Space Program's forces started firing upon the Galaxy Force, moving them to back away a bit from direct aim at the back door. Then the Secret Space people moved in to take control of the door no matter what the cost. It was a full direct assault. The time to leave was now.

Brand's group started running to the right and away from the building. There was a row of shuttles just 50 yards from their current position. They had a double row at the back, and after a few yards from the door, the last row of Brand's group turned to face the Galaxy Force. There were the Secret Space force behind them, with the enemy close in front of them.

They started to fire with a full clip mentality. They were making their last stand. It didn't last long, but in intense combat situations, a few extra seconds can make the difference.

By this time, the Galaxy Forces were re-assembling from either side of the building and heading towards the shuttles. The Secret Space Force was now being overrun by the sheer numbers of opponents. They were good soldiers and provided cover as Brand's group was escaping. They were taking heavy losses.

When they were close to the shuttles, there were six circular crafts with the doors open. Left were only four from Brand's group after their escape. During the run, there was no time to take a count. They were running for their lives, and not until the shuttles were close enough did Brand take a head count. They lost more than half their group, yet now was not the time to mourn. They gave their lives for the rest to board the shuttles, and that must be honored.

Nina Woodhall was concerned. She had received more calls for Sam and urgent messages in the last few hours than all the times before added together. It was like a world emergency was happening, and if you watched TV or were on the internet, you would never know.

A keen eye could tell that many flights were going to certain spots. Private flights, as the ones in the know, were heading underground. Nothing was released to the public. Maybe that was the most surprising aspect. The people that did know weren't telling. They were fleeing to the underground, and the rest be dammed.

Sam was also packing up belongings as he turned to see Nina.

"Nina, it is time for us to get to the command center." He said it with a bit of sadness, yet there was no fear in his voice.

Nina felt for the first time foolish in knowing so little about what was occurring.

She asked, "Did you expect this? Why did you restart this war? I need to know!"

Sam sat down and motioned for Nina to do the same.

He began, "It's a long story and complicated, so I will get to where we are right now, why I restarted it. The SSP split into two factions, one still loyal to us on Earth, the other becoming traders to the Galaxy, their allegiance only to their profit and strength. There was a deal made that while Subject 9 was contained here, Earth would be spared any trouble from all the others out there." At this point, he pointed to the sky and the floor and then swept his arms around the room. It was a very dramatic motion, especially for Sam to do.

Sam resumed, "Once Subject 9 dies, that would end Earth's protection, but while he is alive, he might be the key to stopping the inevitable." Now Sam was getting excited, a characteristic he rarely showed. "Also, while we still have some control over the SSP with Subject 9 doing what he does best, causing havoc to his enemies, well, it was now or never. When he went to Mars, he was ID'd, and the rest was left to fate. It is going exactly as I imagined it would for the victory to be ours."

Nina, now looking like he was mad, "What victory is that?"

Sam having a stern look, said, "Keeping GC from owning Earth!"

Time has a way of making enemies into friends or friends into enemies. Even though time does nothing, everything around it changes. Now the time had come for the Galaxy to choose sides. On the one side, the best company the Galaxy has ever experienced. Making so many things better and speedier. The downside was the control that company eventually had over the planets and people it serviced. The other side rejecting whatever benefits it may receive to maintain its independence. Knowing that if it did not stop soon, that company would win just by the nature of time.

That moment of choice is when big decisions have to be made. Many times it is not anticipated but an impulsive reaction to time and events taking place.

Chapter 45

A BUMPY RIDE

Brand got on the closest shuttle, but it did not immediately take off. It waited, and the six shuttles all rose and left together. They formed a similar formation as their run to the shuttles. Brand's shuttle was in the center, with two in front and three behind.

Once they had entered space, the attack on the shuttles began. The shuttle commanders were well-skilled and made some incredible moves. Even more impressive was they did it in formation.

Even with their great skill, they were being picked off. The number of ships chasing them had to be about 15 though it was impossible to really count. First one and then the second ships behind them exploded. At that point, the two ships in the front performed a 180-degree turn and went on the attack. Now there was nothing in front of them but space.

Black empty space, it appeared they were doomed. Their shuttle not being any faster than the group chasing them. It was just a matter of time, as most things are. Time would determine how long their chase would last before their end.

As Brand watched the pilot of his shuttle, he could tell the pilot was talking to himself.

"Come on, Come on, girl, just a little more."

Brand was ready for his death, but this man acted like there was a chance. The pilot had squeezed every ounce of power into the propulsion system as their life support had been shut down. Now the air was getting cold and stale, yet this pilot had hope.

It started as a shimmering. It was the complete space in front of their shuttle. From the window, it was all that could be seen. Huge just does not describe it. Once the shimmering stop, the most fantastic ship appear. Yet ship is the wrong terminology, for it was more like a city in space.

The real size could not be determined from Brand's perspective. Its shape was long and circular, with a grey-blue flux between the two colors. It had a glow that surrounded the structure, like looking into a light fog on a rainy night. It did not look human-made, and its mysteries challenged the mind's imagination.

Then without any noticeable movement, a large rectangular space opened, and 32 fighting ships launched from there. The pilots were amazing, forming an alley for Brand's shuttle to fly through while also setting up rows of defense as they passed.

Once the 15 GF ships saw what was coming at them, they turned flying as fast as they had been traveling before, except in the opposite direction. Hunter becoming prey, it happens more than people would like to admit.

With military precision, the fighter ships started to re-enter the Nevermore. First, the ships closest with the remaining ships following in row formation. Such accuracy, when dealing with so many ships, shows the skill of his rescuers.

They landed in a huge dock within the Nevermore. Before Brand had even left the now parked shuttle, hyperdrive was initiated. The great Nevermore was millions of miles from Earth with her invisibility on.

Once the shuttle doors opened, there were a group of people to greet him. They walked to the doorway leading from the shuttle bay. It was a long hallway with hundreds of people lined up on either side. Men, women, young adults, and even children. The man leading Brand was Dakota. He was tall, around his mid-fifties. A strong man, yet his real strength was his intelligence.

As they passed by the people, they had their right arms extended horizontally from their body with their elbows bent. Their forearm extended upwards with their hands in a fist.

Brand asked Dakota, "Why are they doing that? What is the meaning?"

Dakota, with a smile, replied, "You created that. It is a sign of defiance. We have your memories regarding the ten years of service you performed. Once they are uploaded, we will fill you in on the last 30 years. Then you will lead us to victory."

Brand now asked, "Why did you download my memory?"

Dakota again having a bigger smile, answered, "You're orders. You said you had a bad feeling, and this may be useful in the future. We are now in that future."

Finally, they arrived at the end of the hallway, where there was a man in his mid-forties. Kobe was his name.

He gave Brand the fist-up salute and said, "Captain Wright, the Nevermore is back in your command!"

When Bubba awoke from a very deep sleep, he felt like it was all a dream. It had taken a few moments before everything that happened the prior day became real. He left his room which was the nicest room he had ever stayed in.

He thought that if he did ever get back to Earth, assuming it was still as it was when he left, that no one would believe his story. Then he thought about what Brand had said before their first mission to Antarctica.

In his mind, hearing Brand say, "Bubba, once you do things like this, you will never be the same." At the time, he imagined how that change would feel, what it would be like. He believed he would feel stronger or smarter, that it would make him braver. But that wasn't how he felt.

Yet there was no denying he was different. Now having a perspective that was awakened. Realizing the ocean, he thought he knew was just a puddle. Everything that was really real lived outside that puddle, feeling he had so much to learn. Also that the truths he now knows could not be described to those who have not experienced life outside or inside of Earth.

He wondered if he would ever see Brand again. Dragonfly said she was going to take him on tour before going back to Earth. He now felt like a little kid excited about going on a field trip, having no rush to get back home.

Chapter 46

THE CORE

The Core was not going to make the same mistake with Plutoneus as before. He will need to be destroyed, but more than that. He would be used to show the Galaxy their absolutism! A public execution with great pain. To the Core it was almost like a gift to their enemy, giving this form of death.

Before they began to own the Galaxy by trade, they were a people that valued the concept of eminent domain. But in their case, not for public use but their own. The phrase, "might makes right," was how they lived. After centuries they learned there were much easier ways to control things.

Deep down, they still longed for the battles their ancestors had. That type of glory can only be gotten when you have destroyed your enemy. It has to be done by hand, similar to the American Indians that would only receive an eagle's feather with a kill using their hands to perform the act.

The Core decided that they needed new strategies to accomplish Plutoneus demise. They would give this project to their military division and provide no overview or controls on their execution. The only requirement was that he be brought in alive so he could be killed in a most painful public manner. Their military division was a violent, sadistic group which were usually controlled in their approach to their missions. Given the military perspective, they could care less about the commercial aspects and cost Galaxy Corp much in profits.

Max was what he was called for his complete name had three very long names, which were hard to say even in his own language. He was larger than his kind in size, smarter in intelligence and most important for his profession, extremely malevolent.

Max was put in charge of capturing Plutoneus with almost no restrictions and unlimited resources. It was as if the Universe itself had chosen him for this great honor. His mind, which was very devious, started to work on many different plans.

Plutoneus was not that tough, nor strong or smart. These are the thoughts Max had when concerning his opponent. He did acknowledge that he was lucky, luckier than anyone has the right to be. Given the right planning, a trap can be designed where no matter how much luck Plutoneus has, it won't be enough.

The Galaxy Corp had started to give surnames to only a few but very important people. All planets and people will need to address them properly and treat them accordingly. Max was promised that surname if he completed his mission with honor. He liked the sound of "Star-Max" once this mission was accomplished.

Chapter 47

NEW BEGINNING

Dakota helped Brand in regaining his memories. They went to the medical center, and he was strapped into a chair. They put what looked like a ski cap but was thicker on his head which covered his ears. Each year would take about an hour plus, so the complete transfer taking around 11 hours. Dakota warned him that he would have a headache and they would complete the briefing regarding the 30 years after Brand had a good night's sleep.

The headache was a server migraine, and after doubling up on aspirins plus seven good hours of sleep, Brand was ready for a history lesson.

Dakota started, "Now that you're caught up on your lost years, here is what followed. As you know, our mission started by helping others while not hurting innocent people. The reality was it was easy pickings, and the Nevermore- well, really you and the Nevermore created a following everywhere you went. The Liberators, as they are called, have had mixed success, yet 30 years later, there are still pockets of their resistance.

About 20% of the planets are with us, or at least not against us. There is a sort of stalemate with a line in the Galaxy. We protect more or less 20% of the Galaxy. GF has held back in breaching that area. Our defenses are strong there, but it can only be held for so long. Time will eventually be working against us. GC keeps getting stronger and building its resources, especially its military.

We need a new direction, something to tip the balance in our favor. There-"

At that moment, Dakota was interrupted by his phone, which Brand imagined by the ring tone, meant it was very important.

Nina had expectations that the command center would look nicer. It had plenty of the highest technologies within, but the walls and floors were roughly finished. There were multiple conference rooms with Sam and a group of men in one of them.

She caught Sam's glance and his wave for her to enter. All the men stopped talking, giving her and Sam a dirty look.

Before anyone could speak, Sam asserted, "She stays!"

Then the man who was confronting Sam replied, "This is exactly what we are talking about, your judgment. It's time to resign."

Sam, hardly breathing, said, "No."

Then another man said in anger, "Why would you send him to Mars, knowing he will get caught? Now we are hiding here-"

Before he could finish, there was a knock at the door with a soldier giving some paperwork to one of the men.

That man started, "Gentleman, there is an armada of alien ships, some friendly but most hostile. We believe they are going to try to destroy Earth. We have contacted all our defense forces which are ready and waiting for orders. That includes all planet defenses plus the SSP forces. Also, we have contacted our other friends for any help they can provide."

If the mood was dark before, it was pitch black now. It seemed like the people in that room wanted to kill Sam.

Then the man who was reading the paperwork stopped putting it on the table.

He began again, "I suggest we all leave the planet. Earth may be the next asteroid belt."

With that, two men jumped up, with the other three men just staring at Sam.

One of those men asked, "Sam, please explain why you have done this. I believe you owe us at least that!"

Sam had been perfectly still the entire time. He looked sad and weary.

"I don't expect you..." and with that paused a long moment, "Men will have the vision or perspective to understand, yet I will put it in the most simplistic terms. If Galaxy Corp takes over Earth, which, if we do nothing, will happen. All of you will be jobless. Galaxy Corp wanted Brand Wright and the Nevermore dead. Yet after years, they failed every time. With all their resources and reach, not only could they not kill him, but he started a revolution that is still alive 30 years later. GC made a deal cause they were so afraid of Brand that to have him sidelined was a win for them. We have the strongest weapon to use against them, and you don't want me to use it?"

At this point, he waited to see their responses and continued.

"It has been asked that if you could go to Germany and kill Hitler before his rise to power and save millions would you do it? Well, I ask you, would you take a bullet to save a billion people? Are you aware of how many planets in our Galaxy have humans just like us? There are thousands and thousands of planets with collectively trillions of people. Is 7 billion worth saving trillions of people?" Again he stopped to look at his audience and continued.

"Brand Wright is not even human. At this point, he is a hybrid, a very powerful one. GC couldn't kill him. I tried to kill him with a very powerful smart missile and failed. He has more combat experience than you can imagine. He destroyed the base in Antarctica and escaped without a scratch. You have never been face-to-face with him. Nina and I have. He is a force when you're in his presence. So with that said, no, I will not be running away."

Now one of the men asked, "So what do you propose to do?"

Sam settling back to his normal self, "Help him if I can!"

The attack on Mars ended as quickly as it began. Once Brand was no longer in the area, peace returned. Their domes had been destroyed, yet most people survived. Many of the buildings were built air-tight for emergencies, just like the one they were experiencing. Some were leaving for safer planets, while others were already working on repairs. Supplies were being delivered, and the feeling was the base would survive.

Chapter 48

THE MESSAGE

Dragonfly had just heard the message sent out on the Galactic newsfeed. She was not going to inform Bubba about it. His excitement about the tour she promised him was refreshing. Showing someone new things and re-experiencing their awe brings back memories. Also, down deep, she had had enough of his interference in her recent life. She could have killed Sam Smith and had extended life if not for him.

The message was that Brand would surrender himself to General Max within 24 Earth hours or the entire planet would be destroyed. She had noticed the message about two hours ago, meaning the Earth had a good 21 hours left before trouble began.

Her ship was well stocked, and she had a loyal, strong crew and did not need Earth at all for her continued existence.

She felt like a mother to Bubba even though she was his junior in years. His innocence on how things work and dependence on those around him brought out those instincts in her. Also, he had never killed anyone, and to killers, it is like dealing with someone who still has their soul. It makes a difference.

Then she thought of Brand. Now there was a distinct contrast. A dangerous killer who can change personas with the speed of a thought. She wondered if Brand would be able to survive this. Of course, he could run away and let Earth be destroyed. She remembered how committed he was to finding Hector's killer, how he helped her with the Sam issue.

Maybe if Earth were destroyed, it would free him to destroy GC without that baggage to worry about. Brand might just let it go for the bigger picture. That was the thing that made him so dangerous. You just never know what he might do.

After taking the phone call, Dakota's face became pale, and he said he needed a moment with CW, and they would be right back. Brand followed him into the hallway, where Dakota quietly provided the information being sent on the Galactic newsfeed.

Brand replied, "I want to discuss this with our top people right now."

Dakota responded, "Well, that is easily arranged, as they are all currently in the briefing room."

The people in the briefing room were strangers to Brand. There was the former Captain with his science, military, and Human resource expert, plus Dakota at the table.

Dakota started the meeting with the message sent from General Max.

Brand then said, "I want all your suggestions, options, and thoughts on how we should proceed with this issue."

The military officer was first to respond with, "We can hold them off from destroying Earth, there are many friendly ships in that area, plus we can call in our reserves. Also, we could threaten to attack their home world if they proceed."

The science officer then stated, "Well, you're not going to surrender to them, so that is one option off the table."

The former Captain then added, "The Nevermore has much more offensive and defensive weaponry than when you last commanded her. I agree that we beat them trying to destroy Earth which will crush their morale.

Dakota had said nothing, just being fully attentive to all that was said.

Now their Human resource expert ventured in with, "If we defeat them there, it will have a great impact on their confidence and determination."

Brand now looking at the group with disappointment started again, "In this room, I need everything on the table. Do not hold back your real thoughts. I know each of you is the best we have, but you're holding back. Let me introduce two other options that have not been mentioned, and then we will reopen the floor to all ideas on what to do."

Now Brand had everyone's attention as he resumed his speech.

"There is an obvious option that we do nothing and let them destroy Earth. I don't think this ship would need Earth to exist, and with Earth destroyed, they will not have a weapon over us."

At this point, Brand tried to gauge the expressions he was receiving from the group before he went into the much less apparent option.

Now Brand went into a very serious tone and said, "I know you are all dedicated to doing anything needed to win the war, so before I mention another option, I want to tell you a story about the past."

He began to tell the story using his hands and arms to express some of the words spoken.

"There was a man whose country was going to be destroyed by the Turkish army. This wasn't just any army, but battle-tested warriors. Harden men who not only saw but participated in the horrors of war. Men who were not scared of anything and willing to do atrocities.

The Count called on his neighboring countries for help, but they refused him. He called on the Church for help, but they denied him. His army was outnumbered more than 20 to 1 against an enemy well-tested. If he did nothing or tried to fight them, the outcome would be defeat. So what do you think he did?"

Looking at the young faces who had no time in their hard life to study history. Even Dakota seemed not to know the storied Brand was relating.

Brand continued, "He went to the first village the Turkish army would come upon. That village had a little less than 200 men, women, and children. He had his men put each person on a pole to die, which by the way, was a very slow death. And then went back to his castle.

When the hardened Turkish soldiers arrived and saw the carnage and how they died, they became scared. They will travel no further feeling if this is what he will do to his own people. Imagine what he will do to us. Their General, who was at the back, traveled to the front line and, after viewing the scene, commanded his soldiers that they were going home.

There is an option that is not nice, but I want all options on the table before we decide on a course of action.

We destroy Earth and blame it on The Core. The galaxy will believe it, especially since they threaten to do so. More important is what it will do to their minds. The Core will know they didn't do it, and we did. If our commitment is that great imagine the fear our enemy will have. Also, it could be used to start a new campaign to recruit more planets to our side."

Whatever they thought of Brand before, it was different now, and that could be seen in their eyes.

Brand then said, "I am just mentioning it as it is an option. Now I want us to really put all the options on the table so the best decision can be made."

Now many more ideas were generated, which went on for more than two hours.

Finally, Dakota looked at Brand and said, "CW, what are your orders?"

Chapter 49

PLANS ARE MADE

Brand responded to General Max's demand over the Galactic newsfeed with the following.

"This is Plutoneus answering General Max's request for my surrender. Your offer is rejected, and I will not surrender. If you destroy Earth, it will be for nothing and bring you only shame. I propose we meet on the planet Latafree. There we will battle, just you against me with the galaxy watching; winner takes all. That will provide us both honor whether we win or lose. I will meet you there in 14 Earth days if you agree."

General Max's response was quick and to the point. He agreed with stipulations which Brand accepted. Earth was saved for now.

In so many ways, things that happen on Earth are also reflected in the Galaxy, or maybe it is the other way around. The news of the big fight was traveling through the galaxy, bringing everyone who is anyone to the event.

There were bets on not who would win. It was assumed General Max would easily kill Plutoneus. The rules were that neither fighter could bring any projectile or electronic weapons to the battle. Strictly hand weapons, with the only power source being the arm that wields it.

The bets were on how long Plutoneus would last. In Earth measurements, would he last 30 seconds, or maybe up to 5 minutes. How long before Plutoneus dies at the hand of General Max? Even though the finale was certain, there still was excitement on how long it would last. That and the combatants themselves. Plutoneus was a well-known name, with General Max also having a following. It was a one-time event with the galaxy eager to watch.

Utago was speaking English, which allowed Bubba to become part of the argument. From what Bubba could understand cause Utago spoke only a few words when he did speak.

Utago was saying to Dragonfly, "I go big fight!"

With Dragonfly explaining, "No, no good will come from you going. It will only last a few minutes, and I am definitely not going to be there."

Utago would not be denied, "I go myself."

Dragonfly, now getting upset, "With what ship? I will not give up my personnel starship." The ship they were on was huge, but there were other ships on board. Most were shuttles, yet one was much larger than a shuttle with space fold technology. Utago wanted to use that ship to go to see Brand's fight. It seemed that after some time, Utago became very impressed with Brand's bravery. This bravery could also be called stupidity, depending on your perspective. That is when Bubba entered the conversation.

Bubba looked at Utago and asked, "What big fight?"

"Plutoneus and General Max."

Bubba mind, now understanding the situation quickly and being on Utago's side, stated loudly and with determination.

"I will go with you!" Then turning to Dragonfly said.

"Please allow me and Utago to go see Brand fight this General, please?"

It was asked with such earnestness, and for whatever reasons, there was a soft spot in Dragonfly when it came to Bubba.

Dragonfly looked like she had much to say and then said very little.

"You both can go, take my personal starship and bring it back once it is finished."

Now Bubba looking at Dragonfly with almost tears in his eyes, thanked her and finished with his arms open wanting to give her a hug. She responded, and for that brief moment, their connection was of joy and sadness. Bubba's joy of being able to go with Dragonfly's sadness of feeling alone again.

Brand made it clear that Sweetbull his blue nose pit bull would have to be retrieved from Earth, that he needed her near him for reasons that cannot be expressed. In truth, Brand had a feeling it was vital to have her by his side. Maybe just the desire to have an old friend near but deep down, it felt like more than that.

Chapter 50

SECRETS

Brand's life on the Nevermore did not feel like home. Trusting people, even people that risked their own lives in your regard, still that feeling of being around friends or family was not there. He spent a lot of time with the youngest members of the ship.

Most in charge thought his plan was suicidal. Any plan would be better. He worked with the engineers developing hand armor. A metallic flexible glove that covers the entire hand, palm, and fingers. This was going to be his secret weapon.

The senior engineer, plus her top engineer, worked on created what Brand wanted. Brand specifications for what it needed to do, how strong it had to be, plus other requirements pressed the engineers to their extreme capabilities.

She began with, "I can't guarantee it will pass any inspections."

Brand looking at the senior engineer with a smile or, more accurately, with a grin, "There is not going to be an inspection. It will just be the General and me on the field with everyone else in the stands."

She had sharp eyes and questioned him with, "How can you be so sure? Even if it works, your chance of not being killed-"

Brand, with the same cocky smile, interrupted her, "I'll be fine. Thanks for your concern. Just get it ready. When do you need to do the implant?"

"Once the weapon is finished, installing the implant won't take long. You realize it can't be removed and may-"

Again Brand interrupted her, "Thanks, I only care about the immediate future. I appreciate all you are doing. Thank you."

Secrets were the commodity Brand used all over the Nevermore. He had the engineers working on his weapon swear to secrecy. Also, the medical doctor who would make him feel like 25 years old, during the fight. He also tried to warn about the side effects, but Brand only had the immediate future on his mind. It seemed like each group was holding a secret from their CW.

Being an undercover agent for a long time trains a person on the value of secrets. It truly can be the difference between life and death.

Most in charge tried to dissuade him from his plan of fighting one on one with General Max. They just could not see the future past the battle. People don't fight hard against something as strong as they fight for something.

Brand had also worked in secret with the communications division to prepare videos for after the fight.

Sometimes in death, a person can accomplish more than all of his living moments. If it played out well, like the vision in his head, this would be the true start of the war.

Chapter 51

THE TIME HAS COME

Words cannot describe the feeling of joy when Brand and Sweetbull were reunited. There is friendship, love, true love, and then above all that, what Brand and Sweetbull had. Their lives being so entangled together with love and need for the other.

For the first time since he left for Mars, Brand was feeling peace. Sure he would have a fight to the death in four days to come. Granted, the chances of his survival were not even a bet that could be made, just how long before his end. Yet with Sweetbull by his side, his emotions were great.

The planet chosen for the event was Latafree, which has great colosseums and party palaces for all types of events. It was really a vacation planet that had neutrality in all other planet's affairs. A place where everyone in the galaxy can go for fine food and exciting entertainment.

Their largest colosseum was already booked but was graciously given for Brand's event. So many from the galaxy wanted to be there.

Places around the galaxy tend to have formats or fashions that you see on other planets. Not exactly the same, having variations yet do resembled places found on Earth. The colosseum being used was a mix between Roman architecture and French Haussmann styles. Being large with highly decorative touches throughout its design. Using marble and granite with fine fabrics, art, floral, and water displays. Its grandeur displaying how proud the builders felt about creating it, which made the audience feel special.

Great news was brought to Brand's attention, there were two people who contacted the Nevermore over what is the galaxy's open broadcast system. It allows people to communicate without knowing their locations. The Nevermore was surrounded by a huge amount of friendly ships, so its location was readily available. It was in the center of that group, being virtually un-attackable.

Bubba and Utago wanted to board the Nevermore and help in any way they could. Of course, Brand approved it, and with three days left soon would see his best friend. The truth was he was not sure why Utago was with him, figuring maybe he was Bubba's pilot.

Brand felt like all things were going his way except for the battle to come. His secret weapon had been created and tested. Having Sweetbull and Bubba back by his side and finding out that Utago was his biggest fan. It felt like it was the Universe's way of saying enjoy your short time left. Even feeling that he felt really good. Going out the warrior's way with friends around him in a huge event was all that he could want if you're going to die.

The leaders of the Nevermore were totally against his plan. The fact that he was Captain made it so he could do as he liked. It was a great feeling, and since he was only putting himself in danger, he had no regrets.

Of course, this was all for show. Neither side would give up, regardless of who wins the battle. Yet seeing two people fight each other for a great prize was like the legends of yore.

It is amazing how the passage of time depends on what is taking place around you. The next three days went by really fast for Brand. Surrounded by Sweetbull, Bubba, and his new friend Utago. Great food and many, many tales were told. Utago apologized more than once for hurting and trying to kill Brand.

Now those were just memories. The truth was Utago was willing to give up his life for Brand. He envied his battle with General Max, how the entire galaxy was watching. Utago was a warrior, and there is no better honor than to fight to the death for a good cause in front of the galaxy.

The event had finally arrived, and it was a glorious day. With the temperatures at 65 degrees and a light breeze, the sky overhead had purple, blue color with shades of orange splashing through at different angles. Truly an amazing sight to see. Brand was observing it while taking in how many beings had arrived to see the show.

There were far too many different types of life forms to describe. He did notice some he had seen before. The colosseum held about 160,000 depending on the life forms' sizes. It was full, with attendees also standing in the aisles.

The field was an oval shape with large square stones completing its floor. There were many announcements thanking many people. It seemed to Brand they were just trying to fill time.

The second level had four large holographic displays of what was happening on the field. The images were larger and had great detail that could be seen by everyone.

After what seemed like a long wait, the announcement was made, and General Max entered the area. The crowd's roar of approval was powerful. It was like everyone there in their own language was cheering him on. It set Brand back a bit. For some reason, he had figured the spectators were split in half for each side.

Then the announcement of his name, or more the name they called him. When the word "Plutoneus" was said, there was an overwhelming cheer that was deafening. Brand now realized the crowd really didn't care who won and were just there to be in the moment. It was louder and lasted longer than what they gave General Max.

That would make sense since he was so outmatched compared to his opponent. Being the underdog strikes a universal chord of pity. Whatever the reason, it was powerful and hyped up an already hyped Brand.

They march up the field towards each other. When they were about 8 feet apart, the crowd became silent.

General Max stood 8 feet high with a wide body. He wore light armor with his arms, legs, neck, and face exposed. The rest was wrapped in a titanium-type steel, being extremely light and strong. He had a long sword and two short swords. He had no shield and weighed in about 450 pounds.

His head was large with a pronounced firm jaw and eyes recessed further back in the skull than a human's. A powerful being in the prime of his existence, also being smart and prone to cruelty. To say he was a scary opponent is an understatement. Even the crowd seemed to be taking in his strength and power, being afraid to speak.

Brand was wearing full armor on his upper body, which was extremely light while still providing protection to almost all his vulnerable parts. His legs were armor free to provide needed movement. He had a spear plus a long sword, four long knives, and his secret weapon. His hands had an armor-looking gloves that definitely restricted movement but did provide excellent protection to his hands.

There are times when logic and good sense go out the window. For reasons that Brand would never be able to explain, he unlocked his chest armor while General Max and the crowd just stared at him. When it was finally released, he threw it on the ground.

The crowd went wild with approval. The sound was overwhelming. There was a moment when everyone was waiting for General Max to do the same. That did not happen.

Then Brand turned his back to the General, walking about 20 feet away before turning and running directly at him, stopping about 8 feet away before he threw his spear as hard as he could. The weapon was slightly off target and only bounced off after hitting the General's chest armor.

In that moment, there was a feeling all had that it would be impossible for Brand to win. Once he was in close proximity to the General, it would be the beginning of the end.

Then Brand began to test how fast the General could move. Compared to Utago, he was not nearly as fast. So for a bit, he would circle the General and then move 45 degrees out of the way when the General lunged at him. At times he was able to hit him with a sword or long knife, but they did not even break the skin that was exposed. His skin had a composition resembling Bear's skin, being extremely flexible, which makes it hard to break its surface.

As everything in life is just a matter of time, Brand's time was running out. His energy was starting to fade somewhat, and the General was figuring out his next move. He became caught. Brand virtually ran into General Max.

Max picked him up with one arm pulling him into his chest. Then with the other arm creating a bear lock and pulling Brand up, so his face met him eye to eye. He made a strong pull with both arms, and Brand's back was broken. It happened so fast that it was like stepping on a small branch with a snapping sound.

Brand knew he had lost control of his lower body. His heart had given up, and soon death would take him. Thoughts about his successes and failures started to flood his mind. Like a picture parade starting from the early years, passing to his first marriage, then his children. Work for the government started to appear. It seemed the pictures were moving faster and faster closing in on the end.

Then the most unexpected thing happened. Some would call it just a freak accident, while the more romantic said it was the power of love.

Sweetbull's collar was connected by a plastic hook, and when she leaped onto the field with all her power, her collar's hook broke. She was now running with all the might she had to her best friend, who was in trouble.

General Max and Brand both turned their heads toward Sweetbull, who was taking great leaps toward them to get into the action. Then while holding Brand with one arm, the General unlocked what had looked like armor but was really a gun. With expert aim, he shot once with the projectile hitting Sweetbull in the left shoulder and then exploding her in half.

At that moment, Brand's thoughts changed. Before he was just waiting for death and had even forgotten his own secret plan. Now, time had stopped again for a few seconds, and the quantity and clarity of his thoughts, plus his rage at what just happened, set into motion the following events.

General Max then gave a laugh as Sweetbull was blown apart. In that instance, Brand thrush his right hand into General Max's mouth. The fingers on each were protected by Steel with sharp protruding blades coming out from the top of each finger, plus the thumb. They cut in with the speed of bullets and had a toxic poison coated on each blade. Not only that, it could then be set to lock into a fist-like grip that would need Brand's arm pulled off if not released by the chip implanted in Brand's head. As Brand used his hand armor his implanted chip controlled the mechanism.

With his other hand being put across the top of General Max's face. Again the blades were ejected, cutting in where each finger was in contact with his face. The hand grip tightened to the lock position. Now the General let go of Brand, but he stuck to his face with Brand's body banging away from the General and back to it again. In each spot his fingers touched, a greenish-black slimy liquid was produced.

Brand was not done inflicting punishment, with his right hand trying to break the General jaw. Unlike the way Brand's back broke fast, this was like a slow splintering until it finally broke. As the tug of war between the General trying to close his mouth and Brand trying to dislodge his jaw, they saw into each other's eyes.

Once the jaw was broken now, Brand wanted to pull it out of his body, but the General skin was persistent in not letting it happen. It was then that General Max realized he had been poisoned and was getting close to death. He had gone down to his knees, still trying to get Brand off his face, but now had a new plan. With the remaining power he had, he rose to his full height and then threw himself with Brand under him to the ground.

As Brand was being raised up again, he used his mind to unlock the grip from his hand, hoping he would fall away from the General. That did not happen as he was too slow, and the General came crashing on top of him.

That blow broke most of his ribs, punctured his lungs, and split open his head. He then lost consciousness.

Both armies that were on each side flooded the field of battle. Each side gathered their hero and marched to their respective areas. If looked at from above, it was like two different groups of ants, each holding their prize above their heads as they marched away from each other.

Utago had thrown General Max off Brand, as he was the first to reach the scene. Then the others flooded together, forming a line with each side's prize moving horizontally from that vertical line.

Each side claimed victory, with Galaxy Force declaring Plutoneus had cheated. The Liberators were energized for the fight. CW, even being old, beat their top General with only hand weapons, wait until they meet their top warriors. No one expected Brand to hurt General Max, the talk was that both had died quickly after the battle.

Chapter 52

BUBBA'S TIME

Bubba's time had come. He thought about, before he met Brand, how he was just an observer of action. Then, after Brand's influence, brought his desire to participate in the adventures. Now his time had come to lead the rescue of his friend.

Bubba had a plan, a secret cure, but he would have to go back to Earth for its retrieval. Most important was to keep Brand alive until his return. This was how he explained it to the former, now current again, Captain of the Nevermore. Utago and himself would go and be back as fast as possible all that needs to be done is to keep Brand alive.

Brand was in a zero chamber, which basically slowed down time. Technically there are miniature black holes that slow down time within the chamber. The doctors explained that he was currently still alive, but his body had taken too much damage. All the internal organs have been ruptured, plus his skeleton has too many breaks to mention. There is nothing on Earth or anywhere else that could save him.

At one point, the Captain of the Nevermore even offered to take Bubba there, yet Bubba would not have it. He remembered what Brand used to say about secrecy. The more valuable something is, the better; less people are involved.

It was compromised that one crew member, Jane, plus Utago and Bubba, would go using Dragonfly's starship. If the Nevermore had to go undercover, Jane would know how to find them.

So the party of three began their quest to go to Earth and retrieve the secret cure to save Brand Wright.

To be continued.

Brad Shprintz lives in Bradenton, Florida, with his pit bull Raine enjoying semi-retirement.

Bshprintz@mac.com

First book: SUBJECT 9 - ISBN 978-1-7371939-2-0

There are so many people to thank that I cannot start naming them for fear I would leave someone out. Yet still, there are some that have to be mentioned. Jason Shprintz who is not only a great son but also my editor. He has written his own book, "The Reverie." Jenifer Shprintz, my daughter, who I am very proud of and who puts up with me, which is not easy. And, of course, Brittany Wilson who created the front and back cover. She is wonderful to work with, and her talents are reflected in the finished product. She can be contacted at https://www.brittwilsonart.com/book-cover-design. Also Roxanne Knies who is a wonderful mother, for your friendship and support in all my endeavors. Mac and Noel Harmon, for your friendship and all the wonderful lunches we have had. And, of course, most important, the readers of my books. There is no purpose without your involvement. I truly mean, from all my heart, that I appreciate your support and hope you have enjoyed this book.